Dani Collins

ONE SNOWBOUND NEW YEAR'S NIGHT

D0100861

HARLEQUIN
PRESENTS

Recycling programs
for this product may
not exist in your area.

ISBN-13: 978-1-335-56830-4

One Snowbound New Year's Night

Copyright © 2021 by Dani Collins

This edition published by arrangement with Harlequin Books S.A.

For questions and comments about the quality of this book,
please contact us at CustomerService@Harlequin.com.

Harlequin Enterprises ULC
22 Adelaide St. West, 40th Floor
Toronto, Ontario M5H 4E3, Canada
www.Harlequin.com

Printed in U.S.A.

ONE SNOWBOUND
NEW YEAR'S NIGHT

To my delightful editor, Megan Haslam, who suggested I write a couple snowbound for twenty-four hours in Canada on New Year's Eve. Writing this romance became its own jigsaw puzzle as I tried to fit all the expected glamour and emotion and heat into that tight frame, but I had so much fun with it. Thank you!

CHAPTER ONE

THE SOUND OF harp strings increased in volume, dragging Rebecca Matthews from a sound sleep to disorientation. It was daylight, the window blinds open to a view of falling snow on cedar trees. How—?

Oh, right. She was back in Canada.

She closed her eyes again and groggily reached to the night table to turn off the alarm. She didn't even recall setting it.

Her hand couldn't find the phone, but the sound abruptly cut off.

"Don't scream," a male voice said quietly.

She screamed, scrambling into a huddle against the headboard, snatching up one of the giant pillows to clutch it across her slamming heart, all while her brain processed that it was Van's voice. She was perfectly safe. He wasn't supposed to be here, but this *was* his house. Or would be, as soon as she signed it over to him.

Donovan Scott, her soon-to-be ex-husband, stood

in the doorway holding his phone in a loose, dangling grip. He wore jeans and a cable-knit sweater and had an even darker, more imposing level of sex appeal than she remembered. That quiet force reached out and wrapped around her like an invisible hand, squeezing the air from her lungs.

She hadn't seen him in four years, not even stalking him online except for a handful of photos her sister had shoved under her nose. In appearance, he had changed only in small ways. He wore a fade on the sides of his hair and had shortened it on top so it no longer flopped rakishly toward one brow. His closely trimmed beard was now shaped with precision to accentuate his jaw and made his golden-brown eyes seem even more eagle-sharp. His mouth held the stern tension of gearing up for a race. All of him radiated that familiar bunched energy he'd always contained. He wasn't competing any longer, so he wasn't lean to the point of wiry, but his body was still pure muscle, all wide shoulders and long legs and power.

There was something vastly different in his demeanor, though. He had no easygoing smile for her. Rather, he exuded suspicion and hostility and harsh judgment as he held up his phone and drawled, "I didn't want you to hear me downstairs and think I was an intruder."

"Well done," she said facetiously. "I told the lawyer to tell you I was coming in to pick up a few things. Did you not get that message?"

"I did. That's why I'm here." His cool, pithy tone made her heart *thunk* in her chest.

She closed her fist into the pillow. She wanted to bury her face in it. Could he tell she'd been crying? She was a train wreck. She'd had a few hours of sleep and a shower after she landed in Vancouver yesterday, but she wasn't wearing makeup and her hair was falling out of its topknot. Oh, gawd. She inwardly cringed as she noticed the green-and-cream plaid on her arm. She'd pulled one of his flannels over her thin sweater and *smelled* it before falling on what used to be their bed for a hard, ugly cry. Jet lag had taken over and she'd pulled the corner of the duvet across her, escaping anguish and loss by falling asleep.

"I was cold," she mumbled, straightening the collar of his shirt against her shoulder. Definitely not cold any longer. A hot, mortified blush rose from the pit of her stomach at being caught in his bed like Goldilocks. "I thought you were in Calgary?"

"Where's Courtney?" he asked at the same time.

They both fell silent.

When the quiet dragged out and she realized he was waiting for her to speak first, she said, "Her, um, flight was delayed. She was going to miss her connection and I didn't want her to spend New

Year's Eve stranded in Winnipeg, so I told her to stay home."

Becca's first and best Canadian friend had offered to meet her in Vancouver and hold her hand while Becca closed out what remained of her life here in Whistler. It had felt like a horrific imposition to let Courtney fly all the way from Halifax for a handful of rough emotional days and a glass of champagne at midnight, but Becca really wished she had a wing-woman right now.

"I thought you were spending Christmas in Calgary with Paisley?" she asked, mentioning his sister.

"I did."

"Her kids must be getting big." She smiled faintly, wishing she'd had a closer relationship with his niece and nephew, but she and Paisley hadn't gotten on.

"They are."

"I only meant to be here a few minutes, but jet lag…" She trailed off, feeling as gauche as ever around him.

This was so stilted and awful. Latent adrenaline was burning through her veins, leaving her entire body stinging. This was why she'd wanted to come into the house while he was away, so she wouldn't have to face him and the mire of memories between them.

"The lawyer initially told me February. I was surprised when he said you wanted access over New Year's Eve."

"This was when Courtney had time off work. She thought it would be fun to celebrate New Year's Eve here like old times…" Becca's voice faded as her throat constricted. Nothing about this was fun. "It was all organized at the last second."

"You didn't have to work through the holidays?"

"I—" A hard jab of inadequacy struck. Why did it make her feel like a poser to admit this? "I'm not tending bar anymore. I'm, um…" She cleared her throat. "I'm starting school soon. I worked until Christmas Eve, spent a few days with Dad and Ollie—he remarried—then I have a prep course I want to take before the actual classes start."

"Oh? What are you studying?" His brows went up with interest that had to be good manners and little else.

"Lab tech?" She didn't mean it to sound like a question, as though she wanted his approval. Maybe she did. She'd finally found something she felt remotely passionate about. It wasn't particularly sexy, but it meant a lot to her.

"I told the lawyer I could send everything down to you. You didn't have to come all this way." His gaze flickered toward the empty suitcase she'd opened and left on the floor. So far there was only a cotton sundress inside it.

"I need to close out an old bank account and… sign the papers." Finalize their divorce. Release the title on this house to him. Everything could have been done electronically, but… "I don't actually want many of the clothes." What was she going to do with designer gowns and high-end skiwear working as a lab tech in Sydney? "And I was…"

As she remembered why she was here, she pushed the pillow off her lap and hooked her heels on the far side of the bed. Her jeans rose up her calves as she dragged herself off the bed. She shook her legs and brushed her bottom as she got to her feet, then folded his flannel across herself, more from defensiveness than chill.

She didn't want to admit she'd paid high-season airfare and come all this way to find a cheap gold locket her mother had given her. Wanda had started wearing hers after Mum passed and Becca was angry with herself that she'd left hers here.

It was Van's fault. He'd started buying her earrings with precious stones and a tennis bracelet and art deco pendants on links of white gold. A modest gold locket didn't go with the sort of upscale designer names his family wore. She would have told him to send the locket to her if she had known where she had left it, but she couldn't recall the last time she'd worn it.

"I'm surprised you haven't moved all of this into storage." She glanced from the door of the closet, where her clothes had been zipped into garment bags to keep the dust off, but were otherwise exactly as she'd left them.

"I'm at the condo in Vancouver most of the time."

Condo made it sound so modest. It was a penthouse with views of Stanley Park, Coal Harbour and the North Shore.

Van moved to the night table and tilted the bottle of wine she had spitefully opened and poured into a glass, bringing both up here with the intention of drinking it all herself.

"Are you mad?" she asked dolefully.

We can drink it on our fifth anniversary, she had said when he purchased the bottle. They'd been touring Okanagan wineries on their honeymoon. It had been one of the vineyard's select vintages, meant to be cellared at least five years, and had cost two hundred dollars when it was released.

"Depends," he said drily. "Is it corked?" He picked up her glass as if they had been sharing dishes all this time, sipped. Considered. His brows went up. "Worth the wait."

The look he leveled at her put tension in her belly and a cavernous feeling in her chest.

"It dropped me like a tranquilizer dart," she mumbled, and went into the closet where her drawer of accessories had already been mined without success. "Do you mind reaching that shoebox for me? I have a vague memory of putting my old glasses in there with some of my travel paperwork. I want to see what else is in there."

"You kept your glasses?" He'd paid to have her vision fixed shortly after they married.

Her frames were cheap and outdated, the prescription completely useless. She should have donated her glasses after the procedure, but, "Growing up, I was threatened with slow and painful death if I ever lost or broke my glasses."

Her family had been poor. She still was, compared to him. Her sister had told her to let Van ship everything to her so she could sell what she didn't want on consignment, but his family had thought her a money-grubbing gold digger as it was.

No, she had decided. She would let him dispose of the jewelry and clothes however he saw fit. She would divorce him and sign over the house with only a nominal settlement. Irreconcilable differences had never seemed so literal, but they had always been far too unequal to find any middle ground—especially once Becca had learned she couldn't give him the children he wanted.

After privately coming to terms with that hard news, she was working on envisioning a future where she was happy with herself and by herself, not thinking happiness could only be achieved by being a wife and mother.

She was here to draw a line at midnight. New year, new life, new Becca.

Because reinventing herself had worked out so well in the past.

The closet was as big as her bedroom in her new, tiny leased studio in Sydney, but it felt like a broom closet when he entered and stood close, emanating his spicy, woolly, snow-fresh aroma all over her.

He brought the shoebox down and angled it away from them, blew the dust off and tilted the lid open. He looked at her expectantly.

There were her glasses in their cloth case along with a charger cord for a redundant phone, a handful of receipts and some purple, green, and gold beads from a Mardi Gras party they had attended shortly after they married.

Flash me, he'd invited when they'd arrived home afterward, slightly drunk and very horny. She'd whisked off her shirt and bra, then sat across his lap on the edge of that bed while he twined the long necklaces around her breasts before cupping her butt and lifting her onto her knees so he could suck her nipples.

Did he remember...?

One tentative glance upward and she nearly melted under the flare of heat in his gaze. He remembered *everything*. Carnality hardened the sharp angles in his face and sent a golden spear lodging itself behind her navel.

Her skin tightened and she grew so hot she felt scorched. It was mortifying to have desire rise up like an apparition between them, but yearning pinned her exactly where she was. She couldn't escape the way she had completely let him have his way with her that night. Many, many nights, but that one in particular. When he'd urged her to take him in her mouth, she had knelt at his feet and caressed him, listening while he petted her hair and told her in intimate detail what he wanted to do to her.

Then, before he lost control, he made good on his promise. He stripped her down to only those beads and gave her what he'd denied himself, going to his knees on the floor as he buried his head between her thighs and made her scream.

She'd still been panting in reaction when he had thrust into her. He'd been rough, but in a good way, making her climax again before rolling onto his back and bringing her astride him where she did everything she could to take him over the edge.

Van was ruthlessly self-disciplined, though. He was a world-class athlete with ridiculous endurance. In a gravelly voice he had told her how hot she was, how much pleasure she was giving him as he thrust up into her. How much he loved watching her succumb to pleasure.

She had shattered and he sat up, gathering his knees beneath himself while holding her with her legs twined around his waist. She had arched back so the beads sat as a collar-like weight across her neck while he bent to feast on her breasts, drawing forth a fresh, pulsating desire that completely overwhelmed her.

No one had ever made her feel like that—like a goddess. Irresistible. Pure and unashamed in the way she gave herself up to him.

As she grew wild and ready to explode, he brought her up into his lap, so she clung around his neck and kissed him with utter abandon. The beads had dangled down her back and her damp nipples had rubbed deliciously against his hot, hard chest as he rocked up into her.

She'd been mindless. Uninhibited and insatiable. Smothered by his kisses and writhing with him in a way that melded them as close to becoming one as it was possible to feel. Words were gone. In those throbbing, exquisite moments, they were completely attuned, speaking a primitive language all their own.

Culmination arrived, striking both of them at exactly the same time, propelling them into another world where reality didn't exist, only heat and white light and exquisite pleasure. The kind that should have kept them sealed for all eternity.

But it hadn't.

Her awareness came crashing back from that iniquitous memory to see his pupils had expanded so his irises were mere golden halos around black, depthless orbs.

With sensuality weakening her bones, and craving for lost passion snarling like a demon inside her, Becca absently licked her lips.

His mouth had finally softened from its unyielding line. There was a distant pair of small thumps, one barely heard, the other louder and accompanied by the spill of beads.

All she really felt or saw or perceived was the force that pulled them together. Magnets finding their opposite and snapping together in a way that resisted separation. Van's mouth descended on hers as his hard arms drew her body into a firmer fit with his.

Longing and loss and sensory starvation acted like sparks on the kindling that was always there. Always. His mouth slanted and swept and *stole*. She loved it. She gave herself up to him with a roping of her arms around his neck and a mash of her breasts to his chest, dragging herself into him even as his arms closed so tightly around her they hurt.

She was glad for that ache. For those implacable bands that nearly cut off her breath. It was like being caught close after a near-death stumble at the edge of a cliff. *Hold me tighter. Keep me safe.*

His mouth was equally hard as he raked it across hers, plundering as though he'd been starving for years, exactly as she had been. His hands went down to her backside and angled her hips into his groin while his mouth consumed hers, tongue thrusting exactly as it had that night when he'd been buried inside her.

This was the sort of instant lust that had brought them together in the first place. It was wild and glorious—a crashing storm that roared and excited and blew down any obstacle in its path.

It was a storm that had left devastation in its wake.

With a gasp of alarm, Becca jerked back her head and fought free of his hold, shoving her arms between them and stumbling as she stepped on her glasses. They snapped in their case beneath her socked heel.

Van caught her arm long enough to steady her, then ran his hand down his face.

"I didn't mean to do that." He swore sharply and turned away. She saw him make an adjustment at his fly as he left the closet. He kept walking, disappearing out the bedroom door into the hall.

Shaking, Becca knelt to scoop everything back into the box. She closed the lid and set the box aside, moving in frantic shock, returning everything to the way it had been so she could pretend nothing had happened.

That was why she hadn't wanted to do this while he was here. Her skin was tight and hot and prickling. Her heart knocked clumsily around the hollow space in her chest. A lump rose to her throat. Feelings were meant to be felt, she reminded herself, but why did they have to *hurt* so much?

Van had never deliberately inflicted pain upon her, but being with him had been one hurt after another and still was. It hurt to look at him, to feel herself come alive as though leaning on atrophied muscles. It hurt to feel the sharp pleasure of his touch and it hurt to kiss him with such intensity and watch him walk away.

It hurt to be apart from him while still wearing his name.

That's why they were divorcing, she reminded herself. That's why she had planned to slip in, find the locket and leave him a note that wished him well. She had spent an hour picking out the right card to do exactly that.

She wanted bygones to be bygones. She would quit nursing what-ifs and disappointments and blame. She would *not* take fresh recriminations home with her.

Still shaken, she moved out of the closet to the night table and lifted her wineglass in a hand that trembled. She set her lips where his mouth had been.

Don't think of it.

But it was too late. Her mind and body were already alight with the memory of all of the places his mouth had been. All the places she had nearly let him go within minutes of seeing him again.

Hot tears pressed against the backs of her eyes.

Damn you, Van!

Damn you, Becca.

Van stepped into the bracing cold of the veranda off the kitchen, trying to slow his racing blood so he could think about something besides the way Becca had just dismantled his self-control as effortlessly as she always had.

He'd forgotten how easily she took him from zero to sixty and kept him there.

Maybe he'd deliberately blacked it out because it was so lowering to lose a fight so quickly and resoundingly. Against *himself.*

He pinched the bridge of his nose, thinking it felt like a weakness that he'd come here at all. Their divorce was long overdue, and he was ready to finalize it, but he had gotten February into his head and had been blindsided by the email from his lawyer that she was slipping in while he was away.

As he'd packed and climbed into his SUV, he'd told himself he was protecting what was his, ensuring she was only taking what genuinely belonged to her. He was no longer the gullible fool who believed people who were close to you wouldn't screw you over.

He and Becca weren't even close any longer. It had been four years, but unlike his father, Becca didn't come from a long line of people who took things that didn't belong to them. She had never capitalized on his wealth, always seeming uncomfortable with it.

That's what she wants you to think, he could hear his father saying about her.

How ironic that Van had vehemently defended Becca to a man who had ultimately betrayed him far worse than she had.

Actually, it was still a toss-up which knee to the stomach had been harder to get up from. When Becca had told Van their marriage was a mistake and stayed in Sydney, he'd walked away thinking no one could have sucker punched him quite so devastatingly.

Within the hour, however, he'd learned his father had cleaned out the family vault. Van had rushed home to deal with that, allowing his marriage to finish dying of neglect while he raced to save hundreds of jobs, multimillion-dollar housing projects and the corporate dividends his mother and sister relied on.

He had managed to keep a lid on the scandal for a week until he could control the narrative, but the fact that Becca hadn't reached out when it was announced that his finances had taken a tumble spoke volumes about why she had married him in the first place.

The entire thing had been a scathing reminder of something he'd always known, but had begun to think was pure cynicism on his part—that anyone could betray you. In fact, trusting people was an open invitation to be deceived.

Since then, Van had been waiting for Becca to show her true colors, expecting another knife in the back at any moment.

There'd been a whole lot of crickets. Years of silence when he regularly considered starting the divorce proceedings himself, but why shake that can?

A few months ago, the request had finally arrived. She wanted him to buy her out of this house. That's all. She wasn't staking any claim to his various family or personal business interests. She wasn't asking him to ship all her belongings down to her. She would come and take what she wanted before the paperwork was finalized.

It had all sounded too easy and, sure enough, she'd tried to get in here while his back was turned.

To take what, though? The jewelry he'd given her? The art that was valuable, but not priceless? The sexy convertible that was in her name and would cost twice as much to ship to Australia as he'd paid for it in the first place?

He'd ruminated on all of that while driving through ever-worsening conditions, foot heavy on the gas in his urgency to get here.

When he arrived, he'd been sure he had missed her. There hadn't been any tire tracks in the long, steep driveway, only a trail of footsteps that were so filled by the steadily falling snow it was impossible to tell which direction they were headed. He had fishtailed his way down to the house and slid the SUV into a drift of snow that would have to be shoveled away from the garage door before he could put the vehicle away.

Entering the house, he'd seen the envelope on the dining room table and crossed to read…nothing. The card was completely blank. It didn't even have a lame, preprinted platitude about everything having a reason or some other greeting card BS.

He didn't understand how a lack of words had scratched hard enough to leave a mark on the granite where his heart was supposed to be, but as he'd stood there feeling as empty as this card, his gaze had caught on the jacket and shoes in the alcove by the door.

She was still there.

He had removed his snow-covered boots to look for her, calling her name. The door had chimed when he had come in, but she hadn't heard any of it. She'd been dead asleep when he got to the bedroom.

The sight of her struck like a kick in the chest. Lower. Hell, if he was honest, his libido had started revving before he'd left Calgary.

It wasn't like she was naked and lying there all enticing, either. She was wearing one of his flannel shirts, but aside from a socked foot and the ash tips in her hair, he couldn't see much more than the tan across her freckled cheeks. Summer Girl, he'd called her sometimes, when she burrowed into him complaining she was cold. She'd playfully called him Jack Frost and squealed at cold hands sliding under her shirt.

We're too different. It was a mistake.

It had been. He'd come to see that they'd been children when they eloped five years ago, too naive to know better. *He* should have known better. His family's failed marriages had taught him that marriage needed a lot more than an impulsive "I do" in order to go the distance.

Van could live with making mistakes. They happened. He caught an edge or misjudged a turn. The important thing was to learn and recover and do better next time. Making a mistake didn't mean it was time to quit. As long as you were trying, you weren't failing. Maybe he hadn't won every single race he entered, but he didn't fail. He always kept at something until he mastered it and won.

Looking at Becca sleeping for the last time in his bed, however, he'd tasted the bitterness of failure.

Turn it around, he had chided himself. *End this on a good note and call it a successful divorce.*

Maybe it could have been if they hadn't sucked onto each other like a couple of lampreys. His erection was still stubbornly pressing against the fly of his jeans despite the fact that he stood on the porch with a biting wind gusting icy snowflakes straight into his face.

That was how he'd wound up marrying on a whim and earning an F for failure. Becca pulled him off keel with a single, smoky look. It was time to put that firmly behind him.

Except… He swore under his breath as he took in the fact that he could hardly see the lake through the blowing snow.

A sixth sense had him glancing back through the

windows as Becca appeared at the bottom of the stairs. She'd removed his flannel and now wore a belted cardigan over her jeans and snug pullover. The soft cashmere in raspberry pink followed every curve of her knockout figure.

He swallowed and pulled his collar away from his neck, releasing a fresh rush of randy heat.

Inside, Becca glanced around. Her shoulders heaved with an annoyed sigh as she spotted the grocery bag on the floor by the door. She moved to snatch it up.

The more things changed, the more they stayed the same. Milk wouldn't spoil sitting out for five minutes, but she couldn't stand it when he forgot to put it away.

Van slid the door open and stepped inside only to have her squeak and dance her feet, nearly dropping the groceries.

"You knew I was here," he insisted. "That's why I woke you, so you would know I was here and you wouldn't do that. I *live* here," he said for the millionth time, because she'd always been leaping and screaming when he came around a corner.

"Did you? I never noticed," she grumbled, setting the bag on the island and taking out the milk to put it in the fridge. "I was alone here so often, I forgot I was married."

"*I* noticed that," he shot back with equal sarcasm.

They glared at each other. The civility they'd conjured in those first minutes upstairs was completely abandoned—probably because the sexual awareness they'd reawakened was still hissing and weaving like a basket of cobras between them, threatening to strike again.

Becca looked away first, thrusting the eggs into the fridge along with the pair of rib eye steaks and the package of bacon.

She hated to be called cute and hated to be ogled, so Van tried not to do either, but *come on*. She was curvy and sleepy and wearing that cashmere like a second skin. She was shorter than average and had always exercised in a very haphazard fashion, but nature had gifted her with a delightfully feminine figure-eight symmetry. Her ample breasts were high and firm over a narrow waist, then her hips flared into a gorgeous, equally firm and round ass. Her fine hair was a warm brown with sun-kissed tints, her mouth wide, and her dark brown eyes positively soulful.

When she smiled, she had a pair of dimples that he suddenly realized he hadn't seen in far too long.

"I don't have to be here right now," she said, slipping the coffee into the cupboard. "If you're going skiing tomorrow, I can come back while you're out."

"I want to make some of that." He reached for the coffee before she closed the cupboard.

She snatched her hand back and staggered away a few steps, glowering an accusation.

You kissed me back, Becca.

Their gazes clashed before he turned away to dig into a drawer for the coffee scoop.

"Would you like a cup? You're not coming back because you're not going anywhere. We're ringing in the new year right here." He chucked his chin at the windows that climbed all the way to the peak of the vaulted ceiling. Beyond the glass, the frozen lake was impossible to see through the thick and steady flakes. A gray-blue dusk was closing in.

"You have four-wheel drive, don't you?" Her hair bobbled in its knot, starting to fall as she snapped her head around. She fixed her hair as she looked back at him, arms moving with the mysterious grace of a spider spinning her web. "How did you get here?"

He made himself keep his eyes off her chest, but he deserved a medal of honor for managing it.

"Weather reports don't apply to me," he replied with self-deprecation. Otherwise, he would have turned away from many a race before getting up the mountain to compete. "Gravity got me down the driveway and I won't get back up until I can start the quad and attach the plow blade. Even then, I'll have to throw down some gravel for traction. I don't know if I have any." He scratched beneath his chin, noted her betrayed glare at the windows.

Believe me, sweetheart. I'm not any happier than you are.

He thought it, but immediately wondered if he was being completely honest with himself.

"How was the road?" She fetched her phone from her purse, distracting him as she sashayed back from where it hung under her coat. "I caught a rideshare to the top of the driveway and walked down. I can meet one at the top to get back to my hotel."

"Plows will be busy doing the main roads. And it's New Year's Eve," he reminded. "Drivers will be making surge rates moving drunks between hotels in the village. They won't risk ditching their car by coming all the way out here."

"So what am I supposed to do? Stay here? All night? With *you*?"

What was he? A serial killer?

"Happy New Year," he said with a mocking smile.

CHAPTER TWO

BLOODY TYPICAL. NOTHING ever went her way. *Nothing*. Her best friend had canceled, her almost ex-husband had turned up and now she was snowed in here with him? Who wrote this script? Someone with a taste for the absurd, that's who.

"Please do *not* make me watch you do that wrong," Becca blurted as Van started to tear the sack of coffee beans rather than cut it neatly.

Van set it down and lifted his hands into the air.

"Is this what we're doing? Bickering until the snow stops? You could stay in the carriage house if you're so offended by my presence. The heat and water haven't been turned on out there since… Actually, is the water turned on in here?" His lofty arrogance dried up as he tried the tap.

Nothing.

"I'll be back." He detoured to the front door for his boots and jacket and disappeared.

Heaving a sigh, Becca ground the beans. She

was desperate for a coffee after her nap. Her head felt stuffed with cotton. When water began dripping from the open tap, she filled the reservoir on the coffee maker and set the first shots of espresso to brewing, then started milk to steam.

As she scouted through the cupboard for chocolate flakes, she took a quick inventory of the freezer and pantry. There was a bag of stir-fry veggies and she could use that jar of pesto to make the noodles Van liked. That would go well with the steak. There were crackers and caviar, olives and gherkins for an appetizer. The cake mix was only a few weeks past its due date, so dessert was sorted... And she was *doing it again.*

Her mother had catered endlessly to her father. Despite swearing she wouldn't become just like her, Becca had slipped on a 1950s apron with her wedding ring and had fallen into the same pattern with Van.

Is this shirt ready for the wash?

Of course I'll pick up something for your mom's birthday.

You bring home the bacon, darling. I'll fry it up in the pan.

The sound of stomping feet approached the side door.

"Only you could walk sarcastically," she said as Van entered and bent to unlace boots that wore traces of snow.

"I went out to start the sauna."

"Why?"

"So we can have a sauna if we want one."

They used to do that naked. Was that what he was imagining would happen again? Probably, seeing as she had practically jumped him in the closet.

She turned away, embarrassed, but it had always been that way when he returned after an absence. He would disappear to train for a couple of weeks and they would barely say hello when he walked in the door, preferring to crash into each other naked on the sheets. Only then were they ready to talk.

She missed that. She had missed him, she acknowledged with a searing ache in her throat. She had missed this house and feeling snug while snow fell and the excitement of being alive because this one particular human was close enough for her to touch.

"You have that," he said as she finished making his coffee and reached for the sprinkles. "I'll make my own."

A jumble of emotions instantly clogged her throat. Rejection, because he didn't want the coffee she'd made, and a wash of vulnerability because he was being considerate and she had never known how to take it when he did that.

Like her mother, Becca's whole life had been orchestrated around service of some kind. If she wasn't cooking a meal for family, she was pouring drinks for strangers. Becca had gone back to Sydney to help get her mum to doctor appointments and had arranged her sister's wedding because Wanda had been in the middle of finals. She had done the very hard, painful work of ending her marriage both initially and legally so Van wouldn't have to.

One cup of coffee hardly made up for that and it wasn't as if Van had even made it. She had, but she said a humble, "Thank you," and sat down on the far side of the island, thumbing her phone to hide how affected she was by such a small gesture.

A text from her sister Wanda wished her a happy new year and asked,

Did you find it?

Becca texted back.

Not yet.

She could have told Wanda she was staring at Van's extremely nice butt and long legs, but she set the phone aside, never able to ignore him. She should continue sorting through her clothes upstairs and search out the locket, maybe ask him if it was in the safe. Instead, she asked, "How is your family? Is your Mom still with Werner?"

"She is," he said with a note of marvel at the achievement. "They stayed here this summer with his kids." He set the fresh grounds with a firm twist of his wrist.

"Stella and Morgan," she recalled. "How are they?"

"Stella was caught shoplifting in the village."

"Oh." Now she couldn't even mention the locket because that could implicate his adolescent stepsister. Becca had only met Stella twice. The girl had struck her as starved for attention, but sweet. She had a soft spot for kittens and secretly wrote poetry. Honestly, if Stella had taken Becca's locket, Becca was inclined to let her keep it. She knew all about feeling un-special and more of a bother to one's parents than a gift.

As she studied the tension in Van's spine, she tried to make herself ask about his father. She only knew what had been reported online, that Jackson Scott had skipped off to an island in the Caribbean with the company's chief financial officer, taking pension funds and other liquid assets, nearly bankrupting the family real estate corporation in the process.

The story had broken shortly after Van left Sydney. Becca had wanted to reach out to him, but she'd been in a very dark headspace at the time.

Looking back, Becca could see she had probably been suffering depression brought on by all she had been going through. She hadn't been the most secure person in the first place and had become very down on herself during her marriage, feeling like a fish out of water as Van's wife. When she learned about her mother's failing health, guilt had smothered her over being away from home for so long. Learning that she couldn't get pregnant had filled her with anger and self-blame and living with her parents had had its own challenges. Anyone who had moved back home after living away understood how hard that was.

Maybe it hadn't been fair to Van to only give him half the story when he came to see her, but it had all felt too heavy and humiliating to unpack, especially when she'd been convinced their marriage was doomed anyway. She had honestly believed she was doing what was best for both of them. What was inevitable.

Of course, she had second-guessed herself by the following morning, but he'd been on his way to the airport by then. They'd both been caught up in family stuff after that. Time had marched on and now here they were, forced to make awkward small talk while pretending they hadn't locked lips a few minutes ago.

She blew across her coffee, lungs burning.

Van finished making his and sprinkled it with chocolate. He turned to lean against the sink. He eyed her as he said gravely, "I was sorry to hear about your mom."

She looked down, unable to bear his seeing how raw she still was a year later or how affected she had been by his small act of condolence.

"I got the flowers and the card about the donation. Thank you." It had been the last thing she expected. Not so much the generosity of his donation to cancer prevention, but the fact that he'd gone to the trouble when they'd been officially separated and firmly estranged.

"I would have come to the funeral if you'd told me."

"It was family only."

Did that make him flinch? His expression shuttered so it was hard to tell.

"There were all those travel restrictions," she reminded him. And funerals were expensive even when they were small. Honestly, she had feared he would see her reaching out as some kind of effort to get him back. If he hadn't responded, she would have been devastated, so she had thought it best to let him find out through social feeds. "To be honest, we were kind of done with accepting sympathy by then. That sounds terrible, I know."

"No, I get it. It's exhausting when people keep asking how you're doing and the truth is you're terrible, but you have to say, 'fine.'"

"Yes." She lifted her lashes, surprised he understood so well, but she supposed he did. His father wasn't dead, but he was gone. She couldn't imagine people had been as charitable in expressing their feelings about Jackson Scott as they had been about her mum.

Becca started to ask if he'd tried to find his father, but he said, "And your family? You said your father remarried. How is your sister?"

"Also married. Wanda and Cliff had their wedding in Mum's hospice room so it was very small, but it was a bright spot. They're in Bali now as an anniversary celebration. Dad married Ollie back in July. Ollie was their neighbor, always coming over with meals while Mum was in treatment. She and Dad got closer once she was gone. They're a good fit." Ollie nagged Dad to take his blood pressure meds and Dad drove her to her hair appointments, exactly as things had been with Becca's mother.

"And you? Are you seeing someone?"

"What? No." Did he remember that kiss in the closet? "Why would you think that?"

Something flickered across his expression, but he only said facetiously, "We've covered weather and family. 'Are you seeing anyone?' comes next, doesn't it? I thought that might be why you asked for the divorce." He looked aside to find the sprinkles.

"No. I thought it was time. Don't you?" She held her breath.

"Yes."

A cavern opened in her chest. She dropped her gaze back to her coffee, refusing to ask if he was involved with anyone. It would hurt too much to hear, especially on the heels of that kiss they'd shared upstairs.

* * *

Becca's lashes went down and she firmed her mouth as though to hide a tremble in her lips.

Van had forgotten how sensitive she was. He was only speaking the truth and had learned the hard way that secrets and lies were far more harmful than honesty, but Becca felt everything twice as much as anyone else.

"I've been busy with other things and haven't made a priority of starting the proceedings," he said by way of softening his blunt agreement. In fact, when he'd sent the card after her mother's death, he'd half expected it would at least start them talking again, but he had only received a thank-you card signed by "the Matthews family." "But you're right. It's overdue. Thank you for getting that ball rolling."

Her nod of acknowledgment was solemn, her mouth still holding that injured pout. "I thought I should do it since I kind of cornered you into our marriage. You were trying to help me stay in Canada and I left anyway."

An unexpected pang hit his chest. He had thought they had more between them than some inconvenient immigration paperwork, but okay.

"I wanted to believe that eloping with someone I barely knew was romantic, but we were foolish babies who married in secret, like we were committing a crime. We kind of were," she said with a wry smile. "That's how we should have known we were doing something wrong."

It hadn't felt wrong. Maybe his libido had been the one doing all his thinking at the time, but Becca had seemed different from everyone else around him. Refreshingly honest without any hidden agendas.

Perhaps that had been wishful thinking. He'd become far more cynical since, able to see she had used him even if he'd willingly allowed it. At the time, he'd only seen what he wanted to see and she'd kept *a lot* from him.

His mind leaped to what he'd learned shortly before he had hugged his niece and nephew goodbye two days ago.

"Paisley told me she was the one who dented your convertible."

"What? Why on earth would she bring that up?" Becca picked up her coffee mug and shoved her nose into it, earnest brown eyes sliding away from his.

His ire dug in with deeper talons.

"I told her you were here, that the divorce was going to be final. She asked if you were selling the car and asked if she could buy it. She couldn't believe you had never told me. Neither can I."

"Tsk." Becca sat up straighter, shifting in a way that denoted guilt while asking dismissively, "When would I have?"

"When it happened?" he suggested with pointed sarcasm.

"Did she tell you *why* she left the kids with me that day and took my car?"

"Yes." And he was outraged that Paisley had involved Becca in her infidelity, if completely unsurprised. Everyone in his family seemed to think promises and integrity were really more of a guideline than values to live by. "She also told me she tried to *pay* you not to tell me she was having an affair." He'd been about to tear a strip off Paisley for that one, but her son had come in the room. "What the hell, Becca? You don't even like Paisley. Why would you lie to me to protect her?"

"It wasn't my place to start a family row and put her children through a divorce, was it?" She wrapped both hands around her cup, as if they were dishing at a tea party, when she asked with gently raised brows, "Is she happy with John?"

"No. They're separated. That's why she wanted me there for Christmas." His family had more divorces than gold medals and that was saying something considering his mother's career and his own. "Tell me what happened, Becca."

Her mouth tightened and she sent him a glower that was impossible to take seriously because she looked like a kitten pulled off a curtain, indignant and injured at being scolded even though she was clearly in the wrong.

"It's not even interesting." She balanced her cup between two hands and let the steam rise to warm her nose. "Paisley asked me to watch the kids and took my car so I'd have the car seats if I needed to go out. I didn't ask her where she was going, but she came back and said the car had been dented while it was parked. She didn't want you to start asking her questions about it so she asked me to report it and say it happened while I was running errands. I said, 'Why? Were you at a hotel with someone?' It was a tasteless joke, but she got very stroppy and said she'd pay me to keep my mouth shut. I got stroppy and told her what she could do with her money. So it's not that we don't like each other, it's that I had something on her and kept it in my back pocket so she wouldn't be such a cow to me."

"What do you mean?" He folded his arms, having a feeling he already knew.

"Come on, Van. Your whole family thought I married you for your money and they made sure I knew it. That's why Paisley thought she could offer me money to stay quiet."

"Who else treated you like that?"

"Everyone. Your mom loved to remark on the way I dressed and how that reflected on you. Paisley said it was nice that you didn't mind my not working, but…*ew*, no. I couldn't go back to being a bartender or a liftie at the ski hill. That wasn't a real job. Your dad was constantly giving me career suggestions, but what were my options? Tuition here is obscene, especially for an international student. How could

I train for a 'real' job without asking you to pay for it? If I did, that would only prove I'd married you for your money. There was no winning." Her profile was stark as she looked toward the windows where snow and dusk were growing thicker.

"They knew I didn't like the idea of you working late in bars, coming home to an empty house, when I could easily support you." Guilt sat thornily in the pit of his gut. He'd shot down any of those sorts of digs when he'd heard them, but it hadn't been enough, obviously. "You could have told me they were being rude."

"No, Van, I couldn't," she said tiredly. "Any time I brought up any sort of problem, you said I needed to hang on until after the games. Then you would say you had to train and walk away."

"I thought you understood—"

"Oh my God," she cried at the ceiling. "Yes, of course I understood. I saw how hard you were working. Even if I hadn't, it was drilled into me by every single member of your family that you had to be supported and protected. Do you want the real reason I didn't tell you that Paisley was having an affair? Because I wasn't allowed to tell you anything that might cause you the slightest distraction. Paisley laid a guilt trip on me. She said I had to keep quiet because *we* didn't want to be the reason you failed to win gold. Did we?"

Nothing could have lit the fire of his temper faster.

At a distance, he heard the layer of support beneath her actions, but he still grew raw with contempt.

"You're no better than the rest of them," he accused. "For years, everyone else decided what information I had a right to know. Paisley knew Dad was sleeping with his CFO. Mom knew something was funky with the numbers. No one told me." He jabbed at his chest. "*I* wasn't fit to be informed until the coffers were empty and a payroll needed to be met."

Then, yes, it had been *expected* that he would hurry home to sort that out.

His anger wasn't all directed at Becca. From the time he had started to show promise as an athlete, his mother had begun putting up shields around him until his whole family had been keeping him in the dark for months and years at a time. The fact that Becca had played right into that game was galling.

"Secrets matter, Becca. They blow up lives." He clapped his cup into the sink so hard, it cracked. He braced his hands on the far side of the island as he confronted her. "So tell me. What else have you kept from me all this time?"

There must be something, given the way she'd sneaked in here when she'd thought he would be away.

She held his gaze for so long, the air in his lungs began to incinerate and turn to ash. Her eyes dampened and his heart lurched.

He thought, *Wait. I don't want to know.*

"Nothing that matters," she finally said in a voice that was frayed thin.

"Liar," he accused, but there wasn't any heat in it. He dropped back on his heels and crossed his arms, feeling as though he was courting the sort of tailspin that left him tangled in a snow fence, worried he'd snapped a tendon.

"It's true," she said in that awful, emotionless voice. "Our marriage is over so nothing that happened back then matters anymore."

CHAPTER THREE

UNTRUE, VAN THOUGHT, but Becca walked away and he told himself it was far more important to get his vehicle into the garage than press her to tell him things he may or may not wish to hear.

Which proved her point?

He bundled up, but still shuddered against the wind and blowing snow as he found the shovel and put his back into moving the drift from where it blocked the garage door.

It didn't escape him that he'd been grasping on to this coping strategy for as long as he could remember. He had a distinct memory of going outside in his pajamas, winter boots and down jacket to shovel the driveway, just to get away from the shouting inside the house. The sooner the driveway was clear, the sooner his mother would get in the car and take him and Paisley to the slopes.

Of course, once there his mother would meet other men. Van would see her having coffee with someone or she would disappear for an hour. Van had tried to ignore it, but his father would press him when they got home. *Don't protect her. You know who she was talking to. Tell me.*

Sometimes his father was drunk and would grow very needy and sentimental beneath his belligerence. He would accuse Van of letting his mother "take" him and Paisley from him. He would pressure Van and Paisley to side with him. *You missed me today, didn't you? Make sure you tell her that.*

If they were lucky, his father would have gone out and peace would reign for an evening, but even Paisley became a source of drama over time. She hadn't had Van's competitive spirit on the slopes, preferring to make conquests of his fellow athletes. Van had soon learned that his ability to make and keep friends depended largely on whether Paisley was courting or breaking a particular heart.

Those dynamics had been bloody exhausting, ratcheting up as his profile and success grew until he was convinced everyone who was the least bit pleasant to him had an ulterior motive.

Becca had given him a place to land that had nothing to do with any of it. She maintained an arm's length from his family, was only interested in the racing circuit for his sake and didn't care about social climbing or using his money for her own purposes. She hated drawing attention to herself, so the only drama in her world was the occasional drunk stranger who'd been ejected from her workplace.

He'd just started to trust she would always be his island of peace when she had pulled the rug out from under him in Sydney, proving herself as fickle as everyone else around him. Why? What had he done? What had he failed to do that caused her to turn her back like that?

He hit a layer of frozen snow and jabbed the shovel in with aggressive might, throwing the scoop blindly into the growing shadows, working out his anger because, damn it, he *was* angry. He'd been angry with Becca for a long time.

Shock and denial had still consumed him as he had boarded the plane to come home. He'd still been trying to make sense of Paisley's call about his father taking all the money. The brutal plummet from the height of a personal best to financial disaster was impossible to process and Becca's decision to end their marriage had been equally bewildering.

But anger had crept in over the ensuing days, tangling with his anger toward his father, one fueling the other. If his father had set a better example on how to keep a marriage together, maybe Van would still be with his wife. If his marriage hadn't come between him and his father, maybe his father wouldn't have done something so heinous.

Van had told himself again and again that he understood why Becca had had to stay in Sydney with her mom, but ending their marriage hadn't been necessary. He resented her for that. He resented that she had turned him into a failure.

As time had worn on and they remained in a cold war, he had decided his family was right. Even the closest people in his life could treat him as temporary and throwaway, so why allow anyone to *get* close?

He no longer did.

Becca had walked away too scorned and bereft to tell Van what she hadn't had the courage to say when he had come to see her in Sydney. If he hadn't agreed so quickly and bluntly that it was time they divorced, she might have opened up and explained about her inability to make babies, but what was the point now? The last thing she wanted was for him to turn around and say, *You're right. It doesn't matter.*

Because it did matter. Very much. And there were many reasons their marriage had been doomed. Dredging up the most painful one wouldn't make any of the rest easier to bear.

She heard him go outside, and the garage door sounded a short time later. She peered out a guest room window to see he was only brushing the snow from his caked vehicle and pulling it in.

She was still poking through the drawers in that room when he said from the door, "What are you doing in here?"

Flattening a hand on her chest, she said ruefully, "I thought you were still outside."

The house was extremely well-built, that was the problem. Its walls were thick, its floors never creaking. Sound traveled from the great room to the loft and down the stairs to the game room, but the bedrooms were well-insulated and Van moved with athletic grace. Becca tended to get caught up in whatever she was doing and it all made for constant jump scares.

Van hovered in the door, glancing at the nightstand where a stack of fashion magazines had been shoved into its drawer. Melting snowflakes glistened on his hair and a trickle of water made a trail down his temple and the side of his cheek.

He swiped at it, sharp gaze still flickering around as though searching for clues.

"I was looking for something to do later." She elbowed toward the jigsaw puzzles in the closet and drew a romance novel off the bookshelf. It was one she'd read, but she remembered liking it. She would read it again.

"Hmph. I'm going to shower." He carried on to the master bedroom.

Don't think of it, she scolded herself. But how could she not? Donovan Scott was a name-brand athlete for more than his talent and achievements. He was six foot one of finely toned abs, pecs, biceps and glutes. His jawline was chiseled granite, his eyes a smoldering fire of muted gold. Showering with him had always been a lot of working up lather and scrubbing dirty bits until they were both too weak to move.

Intensive heat flared up from her chest, making her whole face burn. Becca escaped memories that were quickly becoming fantasies by going all the way down both flights of stairs to the basement rec room.

It was always a few degrees cooler here. The back of the house was built into the slope of the mountain. There was a walk-out patio with a path to the beach that was covered by the terrace above. The terrace extended far enough out that the patio mostly stayed clear, but the accumulation of snow on the lawn was high enough to block the view of the lake, not that it was light enough to see it anyway. Dark was closing in.

Becca turned on the gas fireplace and started searching through drawers.

Van arrived at the bottom of the stairs a few minutes later. He wore fresh jeans and a waffle-weave pullover that clung to his muscled shoulders, accentuating his physical power.

Her mouth went dry and she dragged her gaze back to the drawer of old remotes and computer cables she was pawing through, coming across a mini Polaroid photo that jolted her.

"Do you feel like a margarita?" he asked.

"Do I look like one?" She closed the drawer and quirked her mouth at her lame joke. She came across to set the photo on the polished slab of reclaimed wood that formed the top of the bar. "How's that for a blast from the past?"

She scooted around him into the small, well-stocked space behind the bar. As she looked for ingredients, she surreptitiously watched his reaction to the photo of her in a black turtleneck tucked under his arm. She was beaming at the camera while he was caught in profile, gazing on her with a wolfish expression.

Courtney had taken it and quietly singsonged, "He *liiikes* you," as she handed off the photo.

Lust. That's all it had been, but boy had it felt nice to be wanted that much. Becca was experiencing a hint of that old breathlessness, probably because that same lust was still alive, if their kiss and her involuntary fantasies were anything to go by.

"You haven't changed," Van said.

"No?" Becca hid how deeply that stung by turning to see what was in the fridge. When she straightened and glanced at him, Van was hitching onto one of the stools, dragging his gaze up from her backside.

"Déjà vu," she mumbled under her breath.

"I can't help it if you have a great ass, Bec. That is your cross to bear."

She snorted, trying to be annoyed because *men*, but she'd privately ogled him several times since waking to find him standing in the doorway of their old bedroom. Maybe lust was all they'd had, but they'd had buckets of it.

It was still a mystery to Becca that she'd met Van at all. Or that he'd pursued her when she'd so clearly been not of his world.

"You *have* to come," Courtney insisted. She was dating someone on the ski patrol who invited them to a party hosted by one of his old hockey teammates.

"It's my one night off," Becca groaned.

"Exactly why you should come with us. There's a hot tub," Courtney coaxed.

Becca did like hot tubs. As much as she liked Canada and skiing and spiders you could cover with a cup rather than a mixing bowl, it was bloody cold here sometimes. Sitting in a bubbling, steaming tub while snow fell made her feel very posh and decadent.

"I'll come for a little while," she relented, collecting her togs.

Becca had been in Whistler for four years, but still didn't have a strong grasp on the national sport or the big names on any of the teams. Nearly every Canadian she knew took to the ice in a beer league so *hockey player* didn't compute in her head as someone who played professionally in the NHL.

As they approached the "ski-in, ski-out" mansion, Becca realized this was less a party and more a who-do-you-know? flex. Any celeb who was in town had been invited. The sparkling lounge was full of people dressed way nicer than her plain turtleneck and jeans.

She quickly hid her cheap tote under the coat she'd bought at the ski swap and wished she'd made more of an effort with her makeup. Her hair was nothing but static and flyaway once she'd removed her alpaca wool hat. She self-consciously smoothed her dark brown waves into the indent of her neck as they worked their way into the party.

"Where's your bathing suit?" Courtney asked as she noted her empty hands.

Becca was *not* putting on her faded togs here.

"I'll meet you out there," she said weakly. "I want to get a drink first." Maybe she knew the bartender. It was a small world and an even smaller town.

She didn't know the bartender, but ordered a gin and tonic. While she waited, a silky-voiced Grammy winner came to stand beside her and said a pleasant, "Hello."

Becca was so intimidated, she flashed a smile and hurried away. She wound up beside a man telling animated stories that made her laugh until he glanced at her, giving her a top-to-toe look while asking, "Who is your agent again?"

He was a Hollywood director and, after she stammered out that she was not an actor looking for a part, she slipped away from that circle, too.

How do I not belong here? Let me count the ways.

She glanced outside, but feared Courtney would pressure her to join the half-naked bodies carousing in the hot tub if she went out to say she was leaving.

Still clutching her drink, she wandered the palatial house, pretending she was looking for someone while skimming her gaze away from any men who tried to make eye contact. It wasn't that she struggled to meet people. Men always wanted to talk to her, but they never really wanted to talk.

A number of framed photos and accolades on the walls of a staircase had her edging down them as she studied them. When she arrived at the bottom, easygoing laughter drew her to peek through a door into a den where a big-screen television was predictably showing a hockey game. A handful of men, all tall and fit, were chucking darts at a board, trash-talking each other as they did.

No women, Becca noted. She started to turn away before they noticed her, but her feet were rooted to the floor.

Goodness. Who *was* that? He wasn't any taller than the rest. They were all six-foot-something, all ripped and in prime health, full of swagger and athletic power. They were all dressed in casually upscale clothes.

One man in chinos and a snug green pullover with the sleeves pushed up shouldn't have stood out so starkly, but he did. He had a star power that made the rest part of a colorless herd. He had an economical way of moving that didn't allow her gaze to leave him and the way he glanced over and pinned her with a bright golden stare curled sensual claws into her.

"Do you want to play?" he asked, practically drawing her into the room via tractor beam.

The other men said things she didn't hear. She shrugged in the most deplorably unsophisticated way while he walked toward her with a handful of darts and offered them.

Her throat went so dry she could only croak, "Sure."

Becca's usual comfort zone was to stand on the sidelines listening to other people share snippets of their lives. If men wanted to flirt with her, they could do so from the other side of a bar and buy drinks for the privilege. Being in the spotlight of this man's attention was painful, but she felt drawn along as though caught in a rip current.

"I'm Donovan Scott. Call me Van. These are some of my friends." He introduced the other men. "And you're…?"

"Rebecca. Becca, not Becky."

"Do you know how to play darts, Becca not Becky?"

"Mm-hmm." She nodded, but maybe the fact that she was so overwhelmed by him made her come across as unsure because the four of them started telling her the rules and coaching her on where to stand and how to aim and throw.

It was a little too reminiscent of her tween years when the boys in after-school club had been mercilessly patronizing, snapping her bra and turning everything into a sexual innuendo. She forgot to be nervous and fell back on the cheeky retaliations she had used to survive that.

She took her stance and deliberately held the dart with its flight forward.

"No, that's backward—" Van started to say.

She threw it so it flipped in the air and stuck into the left of the bull's-eye.

Into the dumbfounded silence, she asked, "Do you know what mansplaining is, gentlemen?" She threw the other two conventionally and hit dead center with two hard, dull thuds.

"Do now," Van had said, scratching the tip of his nose. Then he quickly said, "We're playing teams. You're on mine." He caught her elbow and pulled her next to him.

Her heart swerved to catch up and she laughed over the other men's protests.

The evening became fun. The men accused Van of sneaking in a ringer because they won every game. Becca was in heaven, brushing hands with Van as they transferred darts to each other, standing close and murmuring jokes about strategy and technique.

He made her feel incredible. Lighthearted and extraordinary.

Don't let it go to your head, she warned herself.

She dated, but cautiously. A seasonal town like Whistler had people her age coming and going all the time. The culture was very breezy about hooking up and moving on. She'd been stung a couple of times right after she'd arrived. Young men she had thought genuinely liked her had dropped her cold after a few weeks. She wasn't anxious to relive how naive and insignificant it made her feel.

Van, she learned, was an alpine racer who would represent Canada at the next winter games. His mother was a renowned gold medalist and his father's family had started buying up land in this area before a ski hill had even been proposed. His father now developed properties across Canada, making their family one of the richest in the country.

Between that, and the yoga studio and boutique owned by his sister and Van's constant presence on the slopes, he knew everyone.

Van Scott could *have* anyone.

Becca was confident he had approached her because she was literally the only woman in the room. Everything about him was so far beyond her reach it was laughable, but she still basked in the glow of his attention. She couldn't help it. She'd never had a man with this much charisma act as if she fascinated him.

When he said, "I have six hours of training first

thing tomorrow so I need to get home and get to bed. Do you need a lift home?" she knew exactly what he was asking.

He probably picked up women all the time. She would only be a fresh notch on his bedpost, but the way his gaze sparked with embers that arced to land in the pit of her belly mesmerized her. She was having fun here, but only because she was with him. Once he left, she would be back to feeling out of place and awkward.

She wasn't ready to say goodbye to him. Not yet.

"I should tell my friend I'm leaving," she said with a rasp of anticipation in her throat.

"Sure. Let's go find her."

Courtney had been out of the tub and catching up with a friend Becca didn't know. She was quick to flash her camera at them. As she handed over the snapshot, she whispered that she wanted a full report in the morning.

Becca was blushing as they walked outside, feeling as though everyone knew she was going home with him when, in reality, she doubted anyone but Courtney had noticed or cared.

Van's SUV was already running, snow melting off the windows.

"Remote start," he said, showing her the fob in his hand. "Are you driving?"

"What? Oh." She was so nervous she'd absently started around to what was the passenger side back home. Also, she wasn't used to a man opening a door for her. It felt pretentious to go along with it.

She came to where he stood and climbed in past him, setting her homely bag on her boots, feeling too gauche for words.

He stayed in the open door where the glow of the interior light lit only half his face. "I can take you home. I absolutely will if that's what you prefer, but…" He watched her closely. "Would you rather spend the night at mine?"

"This is my bathing suit," she was compelled to explain, pointing at her bag. "I wasn't planning to go home with anyone."

"I know." He choked a laugh. "I wasn't either. I never do this."

She doubted that, but confessed, "Neither do I."

"I mean I *have*," he joked. "This isn't my first time. Don't worry."

"Just me then."

His face fell with shock. "Are you serious?"

"No." She chuckled at the way he clamped his lips flat and tilted his face up to the flakes drifting from the sky, as though he couldn't believe she'd gotten him again. "I mean it would be my *second* time so maybe you should worry a lit—"

His cool hand cupped her cheek and his head ducked in. His mouth covered her grin, stilling her lips before drawing her into a slow, hot kiss that was *him*. She instantly understood this was the essence of the man. He knew how to hold back and wait for the right moment. When he finally took action, he went all in.

That was the last sensible thought she had because he took her with him on a blazing, wild journey. His hand shifted to the side of her neck and their noses bumped and their tongues brushed. Her pulse throbbed in her throat and her breasts felt heavy and her hand rose to the back of his head to encourage him.

The snow could have stopped and spring arrived for all she knew of time and space, because her world was only heat and his tantalizing taste and an earthy invitation to pleasure. So much pleasure beckoned it was irresistible. She instinctively recognized him and this as one of those things in life that others were allowed to experience and indulge in that she wasn't entitled to have. Not material possessions, but luck and joy and those wonderful blessings that certain people fell into without trying. Such things always seemed to evade her best efforts to grasp them, but she bet he got all the best parts of life without even trying.

"Scott!" someone shouted. "Get a room."

With a sharp inhale, he broke away, but stayed close enough to balance his brow against hers. He breathed a laughing curse against her chin.

"Bad form on my part, doing that here, but I've been dying to kiss you all night. It's these dimples."

He brushed a fingertip against one, then pressed his lips to it. "Too cute to resist."

"No," she groaned, losing her smile. "Koala bears are cute. I want to be admired for my character, like my conscientious recycling and my reliable punctuality."

"Mmm." He nodded with amusement. "Those are also qualities I find completely irresistible." He chuckled and kissed her once more before he drew back. "What I was trying to say before you emptied my brain was that I don't know if I have any condoms at home. I'll have to stop on the way."

Her senses were still spinning, but beneath it was the knowledge that a hard crash would follow whatever soaring heights she achieved with him. If she had any sense of self-preservation, this was a good moment to exercise it and ask him to take her home after all. She didn't want him to break her heart and she knew without a doubt that he could and would.

"Okay," she said.

"What are you doing later tonight?"

Becca's ears rang as Van's voice dragged her from her ruminations. Her heart swerved at the jarring sensation of leaping from the beginning of their relationship to the end.

"Pardon?"

"You said 'déjà vu.' Never mind," he dismissed with a self-deprecating wave.

She finished cracking ice into the blender, scattered thoughts coming together in a realization that he was replaying the way he'd surprised her the next day, after their hookup.

She'd gone to work that next afternoon feeling blue. She had fallen rather hard for him in the course of one passionate night. They'd made love three times, including at five thirty before they'd risen and he'd dropped her home on his way to the slopes. As he kissed her goodbye, he'd said with a wince of apology, *I don't have a lot of time for a private life.*

It's okay. I understand.

She'd been painfully aware he hadn't even gone through the charade of asking for her number. She would be forgotten before he rounded the corner at the end of her block, but she would remember him forever.

Maybe she should have felt more chagrin for letting him treat her as a hit-and-quit, but he'd been a gentleman the whole time, ensuring she was enjoying every second as much as he was. It had been incredible.

Wait. *Had* he enjoyed it? That had been the question that struck like a slap hours later. As her self-confidence had tipped into a nosedive, she had turned from refilling the pub's beer fridge and there he was, hitching onto the stool while asking what she was doing with her evening. She'd been stunned into babbling exactly what she said right now.

"You're looking at it, mate. Here 'til closing." She quirked her brow because it still applied.

"Guess I am, too." He repeated his line with equal irony.

On that long-ago night, he'd added, *Give me a menu and whatever is on tap. Don't let me have more than two.*

When she'd served his beer, she'd said, *You're not staying until my shift ends? I'm here until closing.*

Would you rather I didn't?

It's a free country.

She'd been trying to play it cool. She didn't regret their night beyond the fact that she had thought it would only *be* one night, but there he had been. It was confusing, especially since Courtney had teased her about pulling him

Van Scott doesn't take anyone home, especially not ski bunnies like us. Do you know who his family is?

"Why—?" Becca was still feeling splintered between then and now. Her heart was sheared on all sides, eroded by the time they'd been apart, jagged and as susceptible to breakage as it had been that evening.

His turning up to see her again had been a betrayal of her expectations, one that had filled her with more hope than had been good for her. If he had ghosted her, she would have recovered from a dented ego. Instead she was…this. A ghost of a woman still trying to figure out how she had even been married to him, let alone in the middle of divorcing him. It didn't feel real.

She couldn't look at him as she tossed in measures of tequila, pineapple juice and tamarind nectar.

"Why what?" he prompted.

"Why *me*?" She jammed the lid on the blender and warily lifted her gaze.

He made an impatient noise and his hands opened to turn his palms up on the bar. "Why *not* you, Becca? I have never understood why you have such a low opinion of yourself."

Seriously?

"Look around, Van." She hit the button, making it churn ice with the decibels of a cement mixer. When she released it, she blurted into the abrupt silence, "Look at where I am. Look at where you are. You said I hadn't changed. It's too bloody true."

"I would apologize for the money I was born into, but my dad took all of it," he said with gritty disdain.

She pushed her own hurt aside and asked, "Do you want to talk about that?"

"No," he said firmly, accepting the glass she poured him. "But I did wonder if that's why you left." His gaze flashed up, sharp and hard. Watchful.

"I— We had already agreed it was over before you left Sydney."

"Did we?"

Best to sidestep that one. She poured the drinks.

"I didn't know anything about your dad until it started making headlines after you were home. I got a few things in my social feed and followed up."

"Really?" His narrowed gaze picked apart her expression like a surgeon with a knife. "Mom and Paisley never talked to you about it before it happened?"

She tucked her chin, taken aback. "Why would they?" She'd barely been speaking to either of them.

"I don't know, but it seemed suspicious that you ended our marriage right before Dad's crimes came to light."

"I went to Sydney because Mum was sick, full stop. Once I got there, it was very obvious how little you and I had in common." Becca wasn't embarrassed of her roots, but coming from this house to move back into her childhood home had shoved their differences into her face. Her dad had still been complaining about basics, not begrudging Mum a fan in the sweltering heat, but having choice words about the electric company over the bills. She'd been back to sleeping in the bunk beds she had once shared with Wanda. Her Dad kept up the modest bungalow, but not all the neighbors were as diligent. Some were very dodgy, getting police visits in the middle of the night.

By the same token, even though she wasn't embarrassed of her husband, Becca had played down Van's wealth. When Wanda teased her about her designer sunglasses, asking if they were knockoffs,

Becca had said, "Van gets things like this for free," which was true, but it saved her boasting that he would buy her a dozen pair without batting an eyelash if she asked him to.

She simply hadn't known how to bridge that without her parents thinking she was putting on airs or Van thinking she was using him to better herself. Given his remark a second ago, she was probably right.

"I've never cared about your money, but it's starting to sound as though I'm not the only one with a low opinion of me." *Jerk*.

She sipped her tangy drink. She had sugared the rim rather than salting it and licked the grains from her lips. Beyond the darkened window, the snow was reflecting the colored Christmas lights that Van must have turned on when he'd been outside earlier.

"You do, though," he muttered with a flinty look. "Care about my money. You're getting salty about it right now. *I* never cared about the difference in our advantages. I thought you were smart and funny and hot as hell. Same as me," he said with a fresh dose of self-deprecating irony. "I only asked why you've never seen how great you are."

"Because I didn't grow up surrounded by people telling me that I *was* great, day in and day out," she said scathingly.

His head snapped back and she realized she was salty.

"I'm not saying you didn't deserve to hear it." She wiped up a small spill. "Only that I didn't have a natural talent and even if I did, my parents didn't have money for lessons and coaches and time to stand around watching me race or sing or whatever. I was reminded that I was noisy and messy and expensive and needed to pull my weight. So I did and I do."

She also kept her head down and her needs simple. Simple enough that she could meet them herself. She tried very hard not to dwell on how good it had felt when this man had built her up, making her feel special and interesting and desired.

"I know you worked hard in your own way," she allowed. "I'm not saying you didn't."

"Was he hurtful?" he asked through his teeth. "Abusive?"

"Who? My father? *No.*" She scowled. "He said it as a joke like, 'you costly little blighters better make yourselves useful and fetch my slippers.'" She was compelled to defend her father even though his teasing words had held enough brutal honesty to leave a mark. "He's a bit of a sexist and was always more inclined to chase me around pretending to be a monster than say anything sentimental, but I knew he would kill anyone who hurt me. There were hard times and we knew it, that's all."

"How hard?"

"Not so hard I ever went hungry," she made sure to clarify. "But there weren't any frills or extras.

Dad worked any sort of labor job rather than miss a day's pay, but he didn't have a trade and never had anything that could be counted on long term. Mum hurt her back when she was pregnant with Wanda, so it took a long time before she was able to return to the grocery store. She would get stroppy if I put Dad on the spot by asking for things we couldn't afford and tell me not to get above myself. Or Dad would tell me to get a job and buy it myself."

That was another reason she hadn't told them how rich Van was. She hadn't wanted her family to think she was skipping over the hard work of earning things for herself and living off Van—which she pretty much had been.

"It's totally normal to want what the other kids have, Becca."

"I know." She shrugged. "I also know it doesn't matter that I didn't have those material things."

"Is that what he told you?" he asked with sharp insight. "I forgot that he's really your stepdad."

"*That* doesn't matter," she insisted. "He wasn't trying to be cruel, Van. He just never saw any point in mollycoddling. Whinging doesn't solve anything so he'd tell me to get on with it."

When he had called about Mum, he hadn't couched his words. *Doctor says your mum has cancer. Best get back here to help out.*

"You always said Wanda was spoiled because she was the baby. That's what you really meant, isn't it?

He favored her because he made her. You felt second best."

He hit the nail straight on the head and seemed to pound it home so firmly he nearly cleaved her in half. Her eyes grew hot.

"My father loves me." She looked him straight in the eye, refusing to let him see how badly she was squirming inside. "It's not his fault he struggles to express it. Or that he has a closer bond with Wanda because he was there when she was born. I was five years old when Mum married him. We had to learn how to be a father and daughter."

Be good, Possum. We don't want your new dad regretting that he asked us to live here with him.

"You're being very generous to the person who was the adult."

"Because it serves no purpose to be critical of him," she said with an impatient fling of her hand. "I wish Dad had been different. There. I said it. Does it change anything? No? Shocking."

"You still could have told me."

"As if you had time to hear it! You needed to train, Van. You always needed to train." Her voice died to a murmur. She gulped her drink and the hot-cold mixture of frozen alcohol worked its way down her tight throat to sit like a glacier behind her heart. Like an ice cream headache that encompassed her whole body and made her ears ring.

His own features froze except for a tic that pulled at his cheek.

"I'm not trying to make you feel guilty," Becca mumbled. "You asked why I don't puff myself up. I told you." She set her drink on the bar as she moved out from behind it. "I will, however, be happy to hand you your backside at pool or darts. See? I'm very confident when I have a reason to be," she said over her shoulder. "Let's play pool. I feel like we've thrown enough darts already. I guess you're right. I am funny."

CHAPTER FOUR

Van TURNED ON the stool, watching Becca pull balls
from the pockets and roll them toward the foot of the
table while he pondered the contradictions in her.

In certain ways, she was poised and self-possessed.
The night they met, she had trounced a handful of
men who were used to winning. It had been enter-
taining as hell, and when he had brought her home,
she'd been so abandoned and passionate he'd thought
she had a lot more experience with relationships than
she really did.

It took some time before he realized that Becca
had the opposite of an Achilles' heel. She had one
or two spots where she was completely sure of herself and the rest of her was head-to-toe vulnerability
that felt the tiniest arrow.

She hid her insecurities well, employing snappy
comebacks and deflecting any compliments she did
earn. That had puzzled him until he realized that

she got way too much of the wrong sort of attention from men.

Van had often earned stares because of his visibility on the racing circuit, but he hadn't appreciated what it was like for a woman to get stared at constantly until he'd begun dating Becca. He'd gone out with pretty women before her, but they'd been sophisticated types who knew how to put off a serious don't-touch-me vibe.

Becca was this incredible combination of sensual and approachable, often smiling and flashing her dimples, all big brown eyes and freckles like chocolate sprinkles across her nose and cheeks. Then she was curvaceous as hell. No hiding that sex appeal. Even when she wore a loose hoodie and a slouched beanie, she couldn't walk through a pub without every male pair of eyes touching her ass. Van had often been hard-pressed not to knock some teeth in. It was damned tiresome and he wasn't even the target.

So he understood why she took compliments as false flattery and dismissed them, but he hadn't realized that she had rarely received sincere praise in the first place. He tried thinking back, wondering if he'd ever properly expressed his appreciation for the small things she'd done—picking up protein powder or returning an email—when he'd been consumed by his goals.

Probably the most sincere compliment he could

have paid her was listening when she was hurting, and she was right that he hadn't.

"You're wrong about one thing." He rose from the stool.

"What?" she prompted.

"I wasn't told how great I was." He moved to turn on the sound system, rolling through the satellite channels past the last of the Christmas carols to find acoustic covers of pop songs. "I was told how great I *could be*, if I met all the necessary expectations."

Everything about her softened—her shoulders, her mouth, her gaze. He didn't want her pity any more than she wanted his.

"Training was a double-edged sword." He brought their drinks to where she stood near the cue rack. "You're right to accuse me of using it as an avoidance tactic. A-type personalities like mine are the result of two people exactly like me fighting over who should control the star power they had manufactured. When I was young, I got into a bad habit. If I didn't like what was going on around me, I said I had to train and walked away."

"Get out of jail free?"

"Something like that." He was embarrassed to realize how often he'd done that to her, but even small discord with her had felt too big to manage in the narrow slivers of time he'd had available. He hadn't been looking to date or get involved at all, but he'd glanced up to see her watching him through an open door and— Hell, he couldn't explain it. It had been like those times when he was skiing and operated solely on instinct and muscle memory, completely in tune with his surroundings and following an invisible line in the snow.

That night, the line had led directly to her and he'd been swept along it without questioning where it was headed.

He'd rationalized that it had been his competitive nature coming to the fore, wanting to claim her before anyone else had the chance, but it was more than that. From the first glance, Becca had been more than he knew how to handle. He had never wanted to deconstruct why so he'd used what was available to avoid deeper thoughts.

"Training was a blocking drug," he acknowledged. "You can't worry about anything but keeping yourself alive when you're hurtling down a hill at ninety miles an hour. As far as altering one's mood goes, it's highly addictive." He still missed it, but he also knew that he'd missed important things by succumbing to its lure. "That excuse is gone now. For both of us."

Her gaze flashed up to his with alarm.

He didn't like it either. A restless itch in his chest warned him he was more vulnerable than he had ever been.

"Anything we put off saying in the past because I had one foot out the door can be said tonight. We've got…" He glanced at the clock. "Seven hours and fourteen minutes to say it."

She swung her gaze to the clock and her profile flexed with…he wasn't sure what that was. Anguish? Desperation? Something that made him want to grab her arm as though she were falling off a cliff.

In the next second, she slipped on the blasé expression he recognized as her easygoing bartender guise, the shield she used to deflect whatever made her uncomfortable.

"Then one of us runs into the snow without their shoe?" she asked.

"Then if one of us runs away, that is exactly what we're doing."

"I didn't run away. I went home to help Mum." A guilty sting constricted her throat because Becca had been running *from* as much as *to*, but she didn't want to talk about it.

Hypocrite, she chided herself.

She set aside her drink. "Lag for break?"

The long pause as he ran his tongue behind his lip before he said, "Sure," told her he knew she was dodging the challenge he'd just thrown down.

They chalked the tips of their cues before they both bent and tapped a ball down to the far cushion. Becca's two ball came back to halt a mere finger-width from the cushion in front of them while his was at least two hand-widths away.

"You're such a show-off," he accused.

"I can't help that my after-school club had a table." Plus darts and foosball. She was excellent at all three. She moved to finish racking the balls and rolled the triangle to snug them, then lifted the triangle away.

"Call me old-fashioned, but I don't think children should be taught to hustle."

"It's a life skill, same as bartending. Care to make it interesting?" She came back to set the cue ball left of center and eyed him with a deliberately cheeky up-and-down. "Too chilly-willy for strip, I think. I don't want to embarrass you."

"I will if you will," he dared.

Her brain flashed an image of him with his layer of fine hair across his muscled chest tapering down to flat hips and bare, thick thighs. The tip of her cue wavered.

She straightened and took a sip of her icy drink. "Do you really want to stand there naked while I clean the table?"

"Did it ever occur to you that I used to let you win so I'd have a head start when we moved on to other things?"

She chortled. "Van Scott has never, in the history of an undecided contest, allowed someone to get the better of him on purpose. You go ahead and say whatever you need to say to soothe your ego while you watch me break some balls."

She moved back into position and glanced at him to see if he had a comeback.

"I'm letting you have that one to prove my point."

"Which proves mine."

He sipped his drink, but he was hiding a smirk.

The way he was looking at her was so sweetly familiar, it sent flutters across her heart.

Foreplay. That's what this had always been, because if they weren't fighting, they were flirting. Banter or bicker. It had always been a fine line and they'd always gone to bed rather than get to the root of an issue.

Until they hadn't.

What else have you kept from me?

Becca blocked that out and lined herself up. She didn't have advantages like reach and strength, but she was accurate and had great follow-through. As she thrust her cue and sent the white ball cracking into the one, the bunched balls scattered in all directions, clacking against one another. The four, seven and two all rolled into pockets as cleanly as if she'd planned it that way.

"There goes your socks and belt." She swaggered around the table, pondering her strategy. "I don't want your clothes, though. Or your money. What else have you got?"

"Let's keep to the spirit of telling each other things we should have already said," he suggested. "You want three of those?"

Since she planned to win and wouldn't be backed into saying anything she didn't want to give up, she accepted those terms. She tapped the six into the side pocket and said, "Four."

"Let's see." He scratched under his chin. "I suggested margaritas because cocktails make you chatty and I want to know why you're really here."

"Mate. If you think I don't know men try to use alcohol to get things from me, you seriously underestimate all women. Mine's mostly ice and I plan to let it melt. Try again."

"All right." He waited until she was about to shoot. "I'm planning to sell this house as soon as… What?"

She bobbled her shot and straightened to glare at him. "That's cheating."

"How is it cheating? It's something you didn't know." Such a smug tone. He came around to nudge her aside and bent to smack three stripes into pockets. "Now we both have to cough up three confessions."

"I thought you loved this house."

"I thought you did."

"I thought you could afford to buy me out. If you're still bouncing back from what your Dad did, we can make a different arrangement."

"Are you serious?" He was looking at her as though *she* was underestimating *him*. "Is that why you only asked for half the house? You thought I was still broke?"

"I didn't want to ask for anything. My lawyer insisted. This seemed like the only thing I was remotely entitled to since we chose it together and I lived here more than you did."

"I'm fine, Becca," he said shortly. Indignant. "I had to invest a pile of my own money and things were touch-and-go the first year, but we're back on top. I wondered why you only wanted half the house. My lawyer said not to look a gift horse in the mouth. You can have more if you need it. I can support you while you go to school."

"I don't want your money," she said again, slow and firm and with plenty of tested patience. "I never did."

"That one sounds familiar." He bent to continue his turn. "Dig deeper."

She didn't bother counting or reviewing or arguing that if he refused to believe her about not wanting his money, then he didn't really know it, did he?

"I know you only married me to tick off your mom," she blurted as he shot.

"What?" He swore as the eleven went in, but the white plonked in behind it. He moved to the pocket to retrieve it. "*You're* cheating."

"I thought that's how we were playing." She carried her stick around the table and set the retrieved cue ball.

"We're throwing out unfounded accusations?

Because if that was my reason for marrying you, I would already know it."

"Maybe I should say that you liked the fact that marrying me annoyed your mother."

"Good God, Becca. I was twenty-five, not five. I didn't *care* that our marriage annoyed her. That's different."

"Not from this side," she muttered, sending the cue ball to tap the five into the corner before it rolled across and dropped another ball in the side. "She resented me, full stop."

"Mom didn't want me to have any distractions. Between her and my coaches, my days were regimented down to the last minute. She didn't resent *you*. It was the fact that I was married at all."

"Oh, yes. That's true. She made sure I knew it wasn't personal." She dampened her tongue with a sip of margarita, then adopted her snippiest Canadian accent. "Van is asserting his independence, Rebecca. It's a symptom of the pressure he's under. As long as you don't impact what he's worked his entire life to achieve, you and I will get along."

"And that's why you fell in line and never told me about Paisley or any of the other things they said or did?" His voice was filled with smoldering disgust.

"You *had* worked your whole life toward winning gold. I respected that. I wanted to be part of the team that got you there. Falling in line, as you call it, was the best way I could support you."

"Then why weren't you?" he ground out, voice so bitter she straightened before taking her shot. "If you were part of the team, Becca, why weren't you there when I *won*?"

Becca could have touched down in any country when she arrived to watch Van compete. People from around the world were converging here, so the local sights and sounds were diluted by a buzzing multicultural stew. Plus, her brain was in such a fog from racing back from Sydney, preparing to help her mother through her treatments and dealing with what she'd learned about her own health, she wasn't taking in details like architecture or food.

Van's family had been planning this trip for years. Long before Van married Becca, his mother, Cheryl, had booked a house. She had promised to "find room" for Becca since Van would stay in the athlete village, avoiding distractions and preparing for his races, but Becca couldn't face them. Through a friend of an old roommate in Whistler, she secured an air bed in a jumbled flat of excited fans who were coming and going and didn't take any notice of who she was or where she went. It was exactly the anonymity she needed right then.

She arrived the day before Van's first, most important race—which was actually two runs. She picked up her ticket for the venue, but when it came time to take a seat beside his mother and her husband, his father and the woman he'd brought, Paisley and their assorted children, Becca couldn't do it.

She hung back at the top of the stairs and might have seen his family leap to their feet as his perfect form flashed by at lightning speed, but the crowd went wild and her eyes were blurred with joy. He arrived at the finish line in record time. The second race a couple of hours later put him on the top of the podium.

As she absorbed that he had achieved what he'd been working so hard for, Becca felt tremendous hope. Maybe this was all that was wrong between them. Skiing had been a mistress in their marriage from the beginning. Now that he would retire from competing, they could move forward as a couple and plan a future that would fulfill them both.

As she wove through the crowd to where Van was talking to television commentators from around the world, however, she could see he was still as popular as ever. He had stripped off his helmet and was surrounded by avid fans. A heavyset man lifted his tablet, blocking her from seeing anything but Van's image as he scanned the crowd.

When she moved to where she could see him again, Paisley had joined him. Van was holding his four-year-old niece, looking into her eyes with such a happy, tender expression, Becca's heart stretched itself out of shape. Van kissed little Flora's forehead and Flora hugged his neck. Becca crashed into the agonizing reality that he would make a wonderful father, but she could never carry their children.

She had hurried back to the flat and changed her flight despite the rebooking cost. When Van showed up in Sydney a week later, she told him it was over.

CHAPTER FIVE

"BEC? YOU KEEP zoning out on me." Van wanted to wave his hand in front of her blank stare, but she looked so damned *sad* his heart turned over.

Her lashes lifted and her gaze focused on him, but her eyes were welling with tears.

His heart lurched. He swore.

"That wasn't fair of me." He set his stick on the table and took her by the shoulders, drawing her into him. "You were going through a lot with your mom, I know. It's okay that you missed it."

That old sting of disappointment and dismissal had been wrenched out of him by her talk of wanting to be part of the team. Not having her there to share in his victory had made his gold medal a hollow chunk of worthless ore that hung heavy around his neck. It had taken everything in him to keep a smile on his face as he accepted it.

A week after the closing ceremony, his medals were merely symbols of how much *he* had missed and all the things he had failed to see. By then, he'd retired from the sport that had consumed him, his wife had left him, he'd been betrayed by his father, and he was facing financial ruin. Van had tried to accept that Becca had been going through her own turmoil, but it had been a bitter, frustrating time.

"You were right to be with your mom while you had the chance." He pressed his lips to her hair while he used the other hand to take her cue stick and set it next to his.

As he closed his arms around her, she took a shaken breath and gave a shudder, so rigid as she tried to hang on to her self-control, she was trembling.

Had she cried at all over her loss? If he knew her as well as he believed he did, she had been the one to hug and cater and soothe everyone else, soldiering on through her grief so others could indulge their own.

"It's okay," he assured her, rubbing her back. "I've got you."

A choking sob broke through. Her arms slid around his waist and her fists clenched into the back of his shirt. She began to quake, starting to weep her great big heart out, damn near breaking his in the process.

"Babe." He closed his eyes, wrapped his arms around her and one word rang in his head. *Finally.*

It hurt to hear her cry this hard, but she quit feeling like sand slipping through his fingers. He had all of her in his arms again, clinging and real. He drew her around to the middle of the sectional and cuddled her into his lap. She tucked her face into the crook of his neck and he held her close while she completely fell apart.

He hated like hell that she was hurting, but God, it felt good to hold her again. This was why he couldn't so much as buy another woman coffee. No one fit exactly like this against him, soft and round and warm and firm. No one smelled like this or leaned so trustingly into him.

It made him sick with himself that he hadn't insisted on staying in Sydney so he could have held her like this every time her sorrow rose up to swallow her. Why had she sent him away when she had needed him? *Why?*

Despite Becca's abrupt return to Sydney, Van had been convinced she would turn up to watch him race. He had told her he would understand if she couldn't, but he had wanted her there. Deep down, he had believed she would move heaven and earth to be there.

When he had looked around after winning the most coveted prize in his field and didn't see her, he'd felt slighted. Forgotten.

He hadn't known yet that worse was to come. He'd wrapped up with two more medals and a bronze in a team event, then flew into Sydney. He'd been coming off his adrenaline high and was still in the headspace of self-involvement that competing required. It had all combined to make him defensive and remote, but she had been just as obdurate.

He texted from the airport.

I'll rent a car at the airport and arrive at your parents' house around four.

She texted back, responding lot quicker than she had to any other text lately.

I'll meet you at your hotel.

Bring your family. We'll have dinner. I want to meet them.

He'd checked into his suite, shaved and showered, put on his suit pants and a new shirt, his good watch and his wedding ring—which he only wore for dress because it would have caught on equipment otherwise. His pants were so loose from his intensive training, he had to use the tightest hole in his belt. He was pared down to his leanest form, cheekbones standing out so his mouth was a wide, severe line, his nose hawkish, his muscles confused because he was amped with tension and not burning it off with exercise.

Nervous? That wasn't like him. He had met Becca's family via the tablet several times. He had no reason to think they disliked him, but he *had* married her to keep her in Canada. She spoke about them with affection, but rarely shared much about them. It was past time he got to know them better.

He waited in the lobby and saw her come through the revolving doors before she saw him. He was dying to hold her, but something held him back.

She was alone. Strangely, he was unsurprised. It acted as a type of forewarning, if that was possible. He instinctively grew more guarded, sensing an impending blow of some kind. He wasn't sure why. Becca was the furthest thing from a threat. She was small in stature, had those big, vulnerable eyes, wore an off-the-rack sundress and rubber flip-flops. Her hair was in a ponytail, but fraying out of it as though blown by an open car window.

She was always thinking of other people before herself.

Even before they spoke, however, he started to question why and how he'd drawn her so quickly into his inner circle. He'd learned years ago to protect himself from mind games and heart fractures. As this scent of danger arrived in his nostrils, he suddenly realized how unguarded he was with her. Why had he married her so impulsively? How well did he really know her?

Her mouth firmed with dismay as she took in the marble floor and the live pianist, the fountain and the crystal chandelier.

It doesn't matter, he wanted to growl as he walked toward her, latching onto superficial frustrations so he had somewhere to place the deeper aggravation that was starting to eat at him.

She spotted him and flinched as though the mere sight of him hurt her in some way. He started to draw her into an embrace and kiss her, but she barely let their lips touch before she dropped her gaze to the floor between them. Her hands on his arms held him off drawing her closer.

"I was in such a hurry, I forgot to put on my proper sandals," she noted, lifting the toes of one foot.

Not, *I missed you.* Not, *Congratulations.*

When she looked up at him, her cheekbones wore a streak of stark pink that could have been sunburn or hectic heat or the heightened emotion of an impending conversation he suddenly realized they were both dreading. His gut filled with cement.

"How's your mom?" he asked.

"Sick," she said with a twist of her lips. "Dad's home with her right now. Wanda's picking up takeaway after she finishes her classes at uni."

All good excuses for her to be here alone, but the ball of concrete in him hardened.

"Do you want to talk about it?" he asked.

"Not really." She released him to hug herself tighter. "The prognosis isn't very good. Mum had some health problems when she was younger and the doctors weren't very helpful. It made her reluctant to see anyone so she left it too long…" Her expression flexed with pain and sadness. "She's accepting some treatment, but she reckons when it's your time, it's your time, so she won't allow anything too aggressive."

"Bec, I'm sorry." He tried again to draw her into a hug. "Do you want to go upstairs where it's quiet?"

"No," she said with a firm shake of her head, holding herself off from him. "The restaurant is fine."

Her rejection was a resounding kick in the chin. He dropped his hands to his sides and nodded. He began to shore himself up by thinking of all the things he needed to do in the next hours and days and realized… There was nothing. Nowhere he had to be.

Slightly dizzy, he walked with her down the hall to the restaurant. He told the hostess they were only two, not five. She showed them to a table that overlooked the harbor.

They were seated on the corner of the table so they both faced the window. Their elbows and knees might have brushed, but Becca shifted her chair away to make that less likely.

If things had been the way they should have been, he would have ordered champagne and dragged her chair so close he could have looped his arm around her shoulders.

Hell, if things were normal, they would already be naked upstairs, earning noise complaints.

He offered her the wine list. "Would you like to choose something?"

"I'm driving," she said with a tightening of her lips that was neither smile nor apology.

"You're not staying." A trapdoor inside his chest fell open. "Becca—"

"Let me say it."

"No. *You* let *me* say it."

He saw her mouth tighten and he knew he was blowing it by asserting his will, but Becca usually came around to whatever he wanted. He wasn't used to this woman who had flown back to Sydney while he was in Tahoe, not waiting a few days to talk things out with him. Since she'd been here, she'd become less and less communicative, taking longer and longer to get back to him. He'd blamed the time change and his own schedule, but now she didn't even want to be alone with him. Didn't want to touch him.

He had to grapple things back under control. Now.

"I'm done. With skiing," he added quickly when she seemed to pale. "I'm prepared to stay here in Sydney as long as you need to be here."

"Why?" She was looking at her hands in her lap. "I have to live at home and be with Mum so Dad can work and Wanda can go to school."

"I can help with their bills. Your dad doesn't have to work."

"Don't." Her eyes widened, appalled. "Dad's work ethic is important to him. And he needs to stay busy.

Don't make him feel as though he's not able to provide for Mum."

"That's not what I'm trying to do. I want to help." He wasn't used to feeling useless any more than her father was.

She brushed away his offer and sipped her water. "Why even retire? You just turned twenty-six. You could easily keep at it for another four years and win more medals."

"Easily?" he scoffed. "I'd like to be able to use my knees when I'm forty, thanks." And there was something very irritating in her "go outside and play" attitude.

"Your mother doesn't want you to retire," she noted.

"No one does." Certainly not his sponsors. Between his mother's legacy and his own success, Van had become one of those breakout athletes who couldn't be spotted buying chewing gum without the item going viral.

"What will you do, then?" she asked. "Work for your father?"

"No." God, no. Their relationship had been contentious for a while now, mostly because his father was trying to merge their businesses. Van didn't want to give up his autonomy. They'd had a proper blowout right before Van left Vancouver. He'd told his father he might need to stay with Becca in Sydney.

The word *ingrate* had been thrown at him along with some other choice insults.

Becca was still looking at him and he rubbed his thighs. This question on his next steps had plagued him for years. He had never had a good answer, always putting off making plans until skiing was no longer the dominant weight on his time. The mountain that had been in front of him his whole life was gone now. It was time to consider what would come next. He didn't need anything that would get him more fame or fortune.

"I thought I—*we*—could start our family?"

Becca didn't move, didn't say a word. Her cheekbones seemed to stand out like tent poles under stiff canvas. Her lips went white.

"My timing is terrible. We don't have to, Dec. We haven't talked about it and you have a lot on your plate." He sighed with frustration and dampened his own dry throat. "It's true that I don't know what I'll do, but I have some ideas. I've been thinking about a fitness app." It was very nascent and not something he was ready to talk about. "It's something I could develop here as easily as I could at home. I can buy us a flat near your parents so we always have a place of our own here— Quit shaking your head. *Why not?*"

"I'm not going back to Canada."

"I just said I'll stay here as long as you need."

"Ever," she corrected, still with that tight-skinned expression.

"Ever?"

The anguish around her eyes was that of someone being persecuted beyond what they could bear. "I think you should go home and…get on with things."

"What the hell does that mean?" His heart stalled.

"We're too different, Van. Getting married was a mistake. You know it was."

"No, I don't."

"Then you've been too busy to see it," she said with a frustrated break in her voice. "Once you've had time to reflect the way I have, it will become glaringly obvious." She sent a hounded look to the piano man, who was playing both too loud and not loud enough.

The notes were jangling in Van's head, but he suspected people could overhear them.

"Where is this coming from? We were perfectly fine when—"

"We were not," she said.

"No? Well, that's news to me. Tell me what's wrong. Let's work it out," he said through gritted teeth, growing defensive as this started to feel like the sort of scene his sister staged.

"There's no point." She shook her head, part refusal, part disbelief. "I can't deal with Mum *and* this. I can't." She genuinely looked at the end of her rope. "Just *go*."

This was going to be a bad fall. That was the one clear thought that flashed in his mind. He would dissect later exactly where he had erred and how to do better next time, but in the moment he had to make the split-second decision as to whether he would fight the fall and risk the sort of injury that could destroy his life, or go with it and control how badly he got banged up.

Either way it would hurt like hell, but protecting himself for the long haul was always best practice. He braced himself and let the fall happen.

"Is that really the only way I can help you? By *leaving*?" His chest was so tight, he could hardly speak. "Getting on with things?" he mocked.

She flinched. "Yes."

The server showed up to ask if they were ready to order.

"I can't stay." Becca rose abruptly, looking like she was going to cry.

"Bec." He caught her arm but guilt over his neglect of their marriage and empathy at her situation collided into a desire to cushion her, too. He sure as hell couldn't push her when she was this fragile. "I'll stay a few days. If you decide you want to talk…"

She gave a jerky, noncommittal nod and hurried away.

His brain was so rattled, he might as well have been concussed. He ordered room service and went upstairs where he picked up a text from his sister telling him to call.

It's about Dad. There's something you need to know.

CHAPTER SIX

SOMEHOW BECCA HAD a box of tissues in her lap and a handful of crumpled ones in her fist. At some point, she had stopped crying and was now resting in Van's lap, shoulder tucked under his arm, forehead against his throat, hearts beating in unified rhythm. He was playing with the pieces of her hair that had fallen from its knot. She was warm and safe and her mind was empty.

And, because she wanted this sense of closeness and accord, not the harsh words that caused tissues to be yanked from boxes and old anguish that got crumpled into fists, she angled her body into his. She tilted her face so her lips touched the edge of his beard under his jaw and slid her hand from where it rested on his chest to twine behind his neck.

"Becca," he breathed, body going still while his Adam's apple bobbed in a swallow. "Don't do that."

"You don't want—?" *Me?* Her voice died before

she could say it. A chasm opened behind her breast-bone and she started to pull away.

His arms hardened, dragging her deeper into his lap so she could feel his erection against her bottom. "Always," he growled. "But I'm not going to take advantage of you when you're hurting."

They both were, weren't they?

She searched his conflicted gaze.

"When, then?" she asked with a humorless catch of laughter. The clock was ticking.

He released a jagged noise and there was a flash of hot desperation in his expression, one she'd only seen once before, when she rose and walked away from him in Sydney. It had been the hardest thing she'd ever done and he didn't let her do it now.

He closed his arms more firmly around her and crushed her into his chest as his mouth landed on hers.

Here it was, the whooshing sense of being picked up and thrown into a bonfire of passion. Heat and hunger and elation swallowed her. Craving closeness with him after too long and a ferocious, greedy need to fill herself up for the future. She shaped his shoulder and cupped the bristles of his beard and their tongues dueled for possession of each other's mouths.

It became a battle of sorts. He had always been the one to lead, but if this was all she would have, then she would have it all. She shifted to come up on her knees and straddled his thighs, caught handfuls of his hair and dragged his head back so she could crush his lips with her own. She feasted on him as if he were still hers and would be forever.

He let her think she was in charge. It had always been his habit to indulge her before he slaked his own desires. It made her feel extraordinary. Strong and skilled at making love to him. As if she were capable of conquering him in some way when he held so many advantages over her.

His wide hands shaped her hips and massaged the backs of her thighs and cupped her backside, urging her to rock against the thickness behind the wrinkled fly of his jeans.

She did, undulating while she ravished his mouth until his hand streaked under her top. He dislodged her bra and took possession of her breast in his hot palm, two fingers trapping her nipple in a pinch that sent electricity shooting straight into that place where his fly rubbed.

The hand against her tailbone kept her there as he slouched and lifted into her spread thighs, increasing the pressure. It was sexy and primitive and sent her straight into the sun. She was suddenly trying not to bite his bottom lip clean through because climax had her in its grip as surely as he did.

Her cries went into his mouth and he moaned as if they were the best sounds he'd ever tasted.

She could have wept, she felt so good under those ripples of joy, yet so utterly bereft. It had also always been this way between them. They weren't even un-dressed and he had destroyed her. She had been ach-ing with emptiness for years and even as the latent pulses were quivering through her, her need for him grew a thousand times worse.

She was both terrified and hopeful that he might end this encounter here. She didn't know if she could withstand whatever else might happen if they let this go further.

But as she picked her heavy head off his shoul-der and he began tugging at her clothing, she helped him. Cashmere stretched as he brushed the fine knit off her shoulders.

She pulled her arms free, then lifted them so he could sweep her sweater over her head. She tried to pull at his shirt, but he was scraping his beard across the upper swell of her breasts and muttering, "Mine," before taking possession of her nipple with his hot mouth.

A hiss left her as he pulled her to the border be-tween pleasure and pain and held her there. Her heart thudded because she knew this place so well. Here she ached and yearned and exalted and believed in happily-ever-after. Here, she was just like him, en-titled to all the joy there was in this world.

It was a lie, but she threw herself into believing it. She pushed her hands down his back and caught handfuls of his shirt, trying to scrape it up so she could pull it off.

He twisted, tipping her sideways so she landed on her back on the cool, overstuffed cushions. He followed to press his glorious weight over her, squashing her. She forgot what she was trying to do because his clever mouth made her gasp as he kissed her neck and bit her earlobe and sucked her nipples until she lifted her knee and writhed in abandon.

"You make me so hard. Hot," he muttered, lifting his head to send her a look of amused lust as he finished pulling his shirt off one arm and over his head, throwing it away. His hand went to the button on her jeans. "Do we need a condom?"

"I'm still on the pill. There hasn't been anyone unless—" Her organs twisted into knots, but she refused to ask. *She* had left *him*.

"I haven't been with anyone." For a long, potent moment, he stared at her, gaze blazing with outrage. "Damn you, Becca. Why did you do that to us?"

His hand jerked at the waistband of her jeans, wrenching her zip open before he pushed his hand inside the seat and dragged them off her bottom, taking her underwear so the cool suede of the cushions caressed her cheeks.

There was no "us." Not anymore. There never should have been, but exactly like the first night she'd made love with him, her brain refused to stop something that was too alluring to resist. He stripped her jeans until she wore only one sock, then he ran a reverent hand over her thigh and hip, caressing and reacquainting. His touch slowly made its way to her inner thigh and stroked from her knee up, opening her legs while he slid to his knees on the floor.

"Van." She didn't know if it was protest or invitation, fear or anticipation. Then it didn't matter because white-hot need engulfed her.

He was her *husband*, he seemed to say, claiming her with such blatant intimacy, scorching her with flagrant licks and a touch that caressed and incited and stole deep.

"Van," she gasped again, because this almost felt like a punishment. She wasn't certain she could bear to give herself up to pleasure again, without him and at his mercy. She *was* losing herself because there was no hiding anything as he made love to her like this. He knew she was his, only his, always his. She had to be, since she was incapable of doing anything but melting under his thorough, intimate touch.

When she was at the brink, panting and unable to form his name, he rose over her and jerked open his jeans, pushed them down to his feet without removing them. He used his hard thighs to nudge hers farther apart, and the broad head of his sex slid against her slick folds.

Then he was thrusting in. Claiming.

It didn't hurt, but it was so powerful and impactful she made a helpless, agonized noise. All her carefully constructed defenses against him became cobwebs and insubstantial mist because he was *in* her. Profoundly. He always would be.

He cupped her cheek and the full weight of his hips crushed hers into the sofa, the hardness of him thick and hot and indelible inside her.

"Look at me," he growled.

She dragged her eyes open. His were pure gold.

"Tell me you missed this," he demanded in a voice she'd never heard. She'd never seen him look like this—like a predator who had landed his prey and was catching his breath before he finished her off.

"I did." It was a small confession. She could give him that much, couldn't she?

It hurt, though. She felt walls inside her crumbling, leaving her without protection. She would fall for him again and it would be far more devastating than their first time.

"So did I." That was more of an accusation. He raked the pad of his thumb across her lips, shifted and carefully withdrew before he returned in a heavy, hard thrust that was so thrilling, it was nearly too much to bear.

She groaned sharply.

"That's what we get for waiting so long," he growled. His mouth went to her neck and she felt him sucking a mark onto her skin. The sting only made her body tingle more.

She scrabbled her hands across his naked shoulders and back, trying to ground herself. There was nothing but satin skin and heat and weight and blinding pleasure as he began to move with steady purpose, unleashing his power.

This was sex and lovemaking and that other base thing that was ancient and primordial. It was reunion and goodbye. Celebration and loss. It was all the turmoil between them imbued into one act. Every caress was needed and welcome, but their cries held ragged edges of anger and despair. When she set her teeth against his shoulder, it was an attempt to keep him. When he hooked his arm behind her knee, it was so he could claim her even more thoroughly.

And they fought—not each other, but together they fought the foe of culmination. Of ending. They clung to each other, clung to the climb and the journey, and when they reached the wide ledge that promised ecstasy, they held themselves on the edge of it. They pulled hair and clashed in hard kisses while he surged into her again and again.

But the ending was always the goal and here it was. An abyss opened before them and Becca felt as though they were suspended. Breathless. Eternal.

They held on to each other, held on tight.

And fell, bursting into flames on the way.

CHAPTER SEVEN

VAN DIDN'T LET her up when she touched his shoulder. He couldn't. He had poured his entire soul into her and was wrung out, coated in sweat, trying to reel his brain back into his head while his heart was still rolling like a loose coin.

He managed to shift the weight of his chest so he wasn't crushing her, but he pressed his hips more tightly against hers, sealing his relaxing erection inside her.

Becca made a huffing noise as if she wasn't satisfied with that and tried to reach for the box of tissues. "I don't want to stain the couch."

"It doesn't matter." He wanted to shout it loud enough to cause avalanches up the valley. They had just elevated the act of procreation to performance art. Surely reality could wait until he could keep his eyelids open.

"It matters to me." Her voice was small and stiff with offended dignity that seemed incongruous to the way they were lying here without any claims to pride or grace. His jeans were around his ankles. He was pretty sure they would both be wearing hickeys like teenagers. She would definitely have fingerprint bruises where he had gripped the back of her thigh as he came.

Her fluttering fingertips managed to draw the box close enough she could pick it up.

Van reluctantly pulled a few tissues and eased from her heat, rolling onto his elbow so she could untangle from beneath him. She rose and gathered her clothes, slipping into the powder room and firmly closing the door.

He sighed with defeat and rose to pull up his jeans. He still had his hands on his fly tab when she came out wearing only her cardigan. She clutched it closed like a housecoat and held the rest of her clothes in a ball against her stomach.

She barely looked at him as she headed toward the stairs, mumbling, "I need fresh underwear."

He went into the bathroom she'd vacated and washed his face, then braced his hands on either side of the sink, wondering if he had made things better or worse. He had tried to tell her now wasn't the time for sex, but he hadn't exactly put up a fight.

Because he had really needed that. *Her.*

For long minutes, he closed his eyes, reliving her taste, the scent in her neck, the texture of her nipples in his mouth, the press of her breasts against his chest, the twine of her leg around his and the abandoned noises she had made in his ear. The way she had bucked and shuddered beneath him had been exquisite. Her body had squeezed every last drop of ecstasy from his and he would never again feel that good.

He slammed back to earth.

At least one nagging question had been answered, he thought with a dour look at the lusty color still on his cheeks. He hadn't imagined how good the sex was. Being inside Becca, making her his, was the definition of paradise.

Van didn't look at women as possessions or objects. The women in his life were too strong for him to even tolerate throwback sentiments from other men, but when he and Becca were at their earthiest, she belonged to him. No one else. Ever. Like wolves mating for life.

He stopped on the way back to the pool room, clutching at the door frame as he breathed through that jarring thought. He hadn't found anyone since their separation who even turned his head. There'd been a whistling howl inside him the whole time they'd been apart.

Disturbed, he tried to ignore what that might mean and moved to tug on his shirt. When he picked up the crumpled tissues she'd used to dry her tears and took them to the bin beneath the sink in the bar, his gaze snagged on the photo from the night they had met.

He winced at the naked hunger in his profile, recognizing that for all the upheavals he'd been through since, he hadn't changed either. He was still that man who hadn't been able to lift his eyes off her long enough to smile at a camera.

It had never been his habit to pick up women. While he'd been competing, he hadn't been able to afford the distraction, and the demands on his time had made him a poorly attentive partner. *Clearly.* But he'd brought Becca home that night and it had been as incredible as what had just happened between them today.

So incredible that, even though he hadn't intended to see her again, he'd spent the following day trying to recall which pub she had said she worked at. Hours later, when he was exhausted and was supposed to be at home making travel arrangements, he had sat down across the bar from her and waited for her to finish her shift.

Over the next weeks and months, she had been willing to put up with his demanding schedule so they'd kept seeing each other until she had said one day that her visa was running out. *I don't want to go back to Australia. I love you.*

That was the other reason he didn't pursue relationships. Eventually those words came up and, even though Becca had probably meant them on some level, he had heard what she was really saying with that declaration. He knew what she wanted in response.

I guess we should get married so you can stay, he had replied.

Until then, marriage had been something Van had put off thinking about. Asking her had been as impulsive an act as the rest of their relationship. She wasn't wrong in saying they'd done the deed like a pair of thieves in the night. He had known his mother wouldn't be happy, but what he hadn't realized was how happy it would make him.

Van had *liked* taking control of his own life. There had been relentless pressure on him from the day his mother had strapped a pair of skis on his toddler feet. By the time he'd been old enough to question whether he wanted the gold medals she had promised him, he'd been too deeply committed to the sport, and winning too frequently, to turn his back on it.

He had loved competing and was proud of all he had achieved, but those rewards hadn't come without constant sacrifice in other areas of his life. Keeping Becca in his life had been his one selfish indulgence. She'd been an easygoing respite from the pressure, an escape valve, and maybe his marriage had even become something he had wielded the same way he had his training.

Becca's waiting, Mom. You and I can talk later.

It was a childish reason to marry and he would

have been ashamed if that's all it had been, but he'd been enthralled by Becca. He'd liked being married and the sex had been incredible. It didn't surprise him a bit that they had locked lips within minutes of seeing each other and had already surrendered to passion. If anything, he was shocked it had taken this long.

Where did they go from here, though? One tussle on a sofa didn't reconcile a marriage and that wasn't what he'd been trying to do by making love with her. In the years since she'd told him their marriage was a mistake, he'd come around to seeing it that way himself.

Plus, he still didn't know why she was here. He couldn't—*wouldn't*—share his life with someone who refused to be honest with him. Not again.

But that man in the photo was still inside him, still obsessed with having more time with her. And they only had tonight.

Becca turned from the pantry and gasped when she saw Van at the top of the stairs from the basement.

"Really?"

"I didn't hear you," she grumbled defensively.

She'd been lost in thought, not regretting their lovemaking, but not sure how to react to it. It had been as powerful and deeply affecting as always, leaving her trying to shore up her inner defenses in a way she hadn't had to in the past because she'd loved him and trusted him and believed in his promises of "later."

They didn't *have* later. Which left her unsure whether she wanted to cry or rage or curl into a ball or pretend it was no big deal.

All of this was his fault! When he had dropped her off after their first night together, that should have been the end of it. She had known she would never forget him, but she'd been determined to try.

Until he'd shown up at the pub that evening.

From then on, she'd been in this state of defenselessness and uncertainty. He had disappeared every few weeks to train and she had held her breath, waiting for the blade to fall. Or rather, she had waited for the silence that would tell her it was over. A day or two would go by without a word and she would resign herself to never seeing him again. Then he would text out of the blue.

I'm trying to sleep on a plane and a baby just spit up all over my sleeve.

In some cultures that's lucky. What color was it?

Gross. But thanks. I knew you'd keep me from yelling at a child. I'll call when I land. Gonna try to sleep more.

Or he would text that he was exhausted and having an early night, so he wasn't coming by the pub.

She would interpret it as him pulling away, but then he would text again.

Come sleep here if you want.

He gave her a key that she used when he invited her. Sometimes they would make love when she slipped into bed beside him, other times he would simply pull her close for a kiss and a murmured, "Hey." Then he would leave her sleeping when he left a few hours later to train.

He had never said he loved her, but all of those small things had added up to her believing he did. Or could. Someday. When he had more time.

"I'll cook," Van said, dragging her back to the kitchen.

"Pardon?"

"Is it jet lag? Where do you keep going?"

"Nowhere. This is just weird." She was so acutely aware of him, she felt as though she walked on a bed of nails. She set down the things she'd retrieved from the pantry and turned to find a wall of a man beside her, watching her with his eagle eyes.

"Should we talk about it?" he asked in a low voice.

She longed to play dumb. Her heart already felt peeled down to its pulsating core.

"And say what?" She tried very hard to sound dispassionate. "That you haven't lost your knack?"

"Neither have you."

She could have wallowed in the heady joy of making love with him for the rest of the night. She had wanted to, but she'd slipped away from him as fast as she could out of self-preservation. Their intimacy had stirred up all the embers of passion and hope she'd harbored through those tense times of feeling ancillary and unaccepted by his family and simply not good enough. Not *enough*.

She couldn't let herself start dreaming again. It would make their parting tomorrow all the more heartbreaking.

"It was nostalgia, Van. You think we're the first couple to have one for the road?" She couldn't hold his penetrating stare, but as she dropped her gaze to his wide chest, she only felt despair.

In her periphery, she thought she saw his hand come up, but she was already turning away to fiddle with the jars and boxes she'd set out.

"What's all this? Did you work up an appetite?"

She flicked him a look of rebuke. He had his arms folded across his powerful chest and his expression had become inscrutable.

"My stomach is still in Australia. It's asking why it's lunchtime and I still haven't eaten breakfast." She opened crackers and Parmesan-encrusted *croustilles*, a tapenade of artichoke and olives, pickles and nuts, caviar and shrimp with cocktail sauce.

"All you've had today is wine and a margarita?" He frowned at the clock that would chime seven soon.

"There were muffins at my hotel this morning, but I wasn't hungry." It had been a bargain hotel, the food uninspiring, and her belly had been knotted up with anxiety. It still was.

"I'll start some eggs." He opened the jar of gherkins she handed him and turned to the fridge.

"No, I'll cook pasta and vegetables with the steak in a little while. I just need a bite while I put the cake in the oven."

"I'll make the cake. Sit down and eat." He picked up the mix and frowned at it. "Why do you want cake?" He had always been careful about empty calories.

"It's New Year's Eve." And she loved angel food. "I'll do it." She spooned some caviar onto a cracker and shoved it into her mouth, then reached for the box.

"I can do it," he insisted, avoiding her attempt to take it while continuing to read it. He pointed at the back of the box. "Do I own a pan that looks like that?"

She *tsked* and moved to the cupboard where the mixer and baking pans had resided. The moment she set them out, he commandeered them.

"Maybe the reason you're always on this side of the bar is because you never sit down on the other side. Eat."

Look at where I am. Look at where you are.

"My limitations are all in my head? Gosh, you really missed your calling with the pop psych advice. Thanks." A hot sting arrived behind her eyes and she moved to take a seat, but she wasn't sure if she could swallow anything.

She bit her lips, afraid they were trembling. She wasn't even sure why she was so hurt, just that it felt as though he was saying it was her fault that she felt like everything was her fault. It was circular logic, but it rang true as it churned inside her.

"You do limit yourself," he accused, eyes still on the baking instructions. "You want to argue over something stupid like a cake when you're really mad we had sex. Spit the dummy, as you like to say."

"I'm not mad."

"You're not happy."

"Are *you*?"

"I'm making you a cake, aren't I?" His gaze flashed up, no mockery or laughter there, only molten gold.

He turned his back to plug in the mixer so he didn't see her biting back a smile, rolling eyes that grew damp.

This was why he'd snared her heart so quickly and easily. He was funny and thoughtful and took charge while making her feel special.

Oh, get over it, Becca. It's a freaking add-water cake.

And she wasn't special. Van was a thoughtful man who did nice things for everyone. For all his hyperfocus on his training, he'd never been curt to anyone no matter what had been damaged on a flight or who had been slow to get back to him. He had taken time to speak with any young athlete who had a case of hero worship and spoiled his niece and nephew relentlessly. Even his family, who drove him around the bend much of the time, were people he would do nearly anything for.

Deep down, Becca had always wondered if he had married her as a favor more than anything. Now was the time to ask, but if it was true, she didn't think she could stand to hear it. It would finish her off, it really would.

"I don't think we should put much stock into it," she said when he turned off the mixer. "We both have lives on separate continents. I don't have any expectations as a result." Longings, maybe. Wistfulness. But she knew better. "It was nice. Thank you."

"Nice," he chided. "We both broke a four-year dry spell and doing it on that couch always left me needing a chiropractor, but okay. Yeah. It *was* nice. Thanks."

She smirked at his back while he got the cake into the oven.

After he'd set the timer, Van sat down next to her and helped himself to what she'd left. "Why lab tech?"

"Why not lab tech? Are you going to say I'm limiting myself? I don't have the stamina or the grades to become a doctor. I'd be thirty-five before I could practice. This is a two-year program and most of the second year is practical." Getting the prerequisites had required extra tutoring on her part. She'd worked really hard and was proud she'd been accepted.

"Don't be so defensive. I only thought you'd be put off by anything to do with medical care after going through everything with your mom."

"Oh. Yes. A little," she said sheepishly. "But that's also how I know it means a lot when you find someone who is willing to give you that extra minute to roll up your sleeve or ask a question. I don't blame the doctors and nurses who are trying to help as many people as possible. Burnout is chronic because they're so overworked, but they're also people we need, so health care is a good career sector. I looked at a lot of different fields and thought taking blood would be like serving drinks. People sit down for a few minutes, you listen to them talk about their day or tell a joke to brighten their mood." She gave a self-deprecating shrug. "I'm good at that."

He didn't laugh, only nodded agreement. "You are."

His gaze was narrowed, as if he was putting together what she'd said earlier about pulling her weight with wanting a job that made her feel useful and necessary—which was pretty much right on the nose.

"At least I'll *be* something." She ate one more olive, leaving the last few for him.

"What does that mean? 'Be something.'"

"You know, when you meet someone and they ask what you do. I'll be able to say, 'I'm a lab tech.' They'll nod and that will be the end of it. When I say I'm a bartender, I get a look that implies it's not a real job. People think it's a great job for someone in their twenties on a working holiday visa, but it's not seen as a serious career. Which isn't to say I'm embarrassed I did it for so long or would never make it my career. I'm glad I'll always have it to fall back on, but I'm ready to work daylight hours and deal with people in a different way."

"I never once introduced myself as Donovan Scott, alpine champion, but that's what I was for the longest time. Now I'm CEO of Scott B&D and you should see the looks I get." His mouth twisted with dismay.

She knew the B&D stood for builders and developers, but his expression was so grim at taking over from his father, she had to tease, "Because of the bondage and discipline jokes? Yeah, that has to wear thin."

He closed his eyes in an exaggerated reach for patience. "No one ever makes that joke. Only you."

"How does anyone resist? It's right there." She opened her hands to point at the invisible bowling pin that begged to be knocked down.

"They like to live?" he suggested as he crunched a tapenade-laden cracker and gave her a look of mock warning, but there was reluctant humor beneath it.

She propped her chin in her hand, pondering. "I want to say something about how you should have had a safe word for all the pain your father caused you, but maybe it's too soon?"

"Way too soon," he assured her as murderous rage replaced the lazy humor in his eyes.

Her insides caved in and old fault rose like a ghoul inside her. She had had a lot to deal with when she'd walked away from him in Sydney. Her world had been collapsing on all sides as she gave up her marriage, accepted her inability to get pregnant and faced the loss of her mum.

Even so, she could have reached out to Van when his troubles had started making headlines. She had been tempted to. She had nearly gone back to the hotel to see him the very next morning after leaving him there, still unaware of his father's troubles, but wondering if they could figure something out after all.

She had gotten a text first thing that he was headed to the airport because of a family issue. She had texted back that she hoped everyone was okay and that had pretty much been their last direct communication.

"There was nothing I could do when I realized what was going on," she said, heart heavy as she swiveled to face him. "I couldn't leave Mum and I thought I would just be a distraction if I came back. I honestly thought it was simpler for you if I was out of the picture and you could focus on whatever you had to do. It must have been awful."

"It was." His expression remained shuttered.

"It's okay if you don't want to talk about it."

He ate in silence a minute before saying flatly, "There's not much to say beyond what was in the headlines anyway. Dad colluded with his CFO in a smash-and-grab. They took mortgages on properties that were already leveraged to the gills, scraped everything into liquidation accounts, shifted it all offshore, bought a yacht and *hasta la vista*, baby." He flicked his hand in a careless salute.

"There's no way to catch him and get any of it back? Is he still moving around?"

"Hell, no. He bought a house on an island that has an electrified gate and a couple of dogs that don't like strangers. I buzzed and he refused to see me. I would have settled for an explanation, but he wouldn't even give me that. So I left. Screw him."

"He wouldn't see you? Van." She touched his arm.

He was like iron, barely controlling his fury. He stiffly removed his arm from beneath the weight of her hand.

"He'd been bleeding red ink for years and kept it from the board. I always let Mom or Paisley vote my share, trusting them to be up-front if something was wrong. Mom had suspicions, but she and Dad were always so hostile toward each other any of her criticism was dismissed by the rest of the board as bad blood. Even Paisley didn't take her seriously. She thought Mom knew Dad was sleeping with the CFO and that's why Mom was raising all these red flags. Neither of them brought it up with me because..." He made a noise of frustration.

"Training," she murmured.

"Exactly." He rose and went to the fridge, taking out two bottles from the multipack selection of microbrew beer he'd bought with his groceries.

"We have open alcohol all over this house," she reminded him.

"Not on this floor." He put one back when she flicked her wrist in refusal. He opened his bottle and tilted a squat beer mug to pour. "Everyone expected me to work for Dad once I retired from skiing. Mom and Paisley saw no harm in letting their suspicions slide until the games were over. They had every expectation that I would deal with things soon enough. Maybe Dad thought I would finally merge my business with his and save his ass."

"He was serious about that? I thought it was a joke whenever he said it. I mean, real estate and sports equipment? It doesn't even make sense."

"No, but I knew he wasn't joking. That's what makes me angriest. I didn't ask myself *why* he wanted my money. Yes, Mom and Paisley could have been more forthcoming, but I trusted him to tell me that something was wrong. I pushed aside the suspicions *I* had."

"You can't blame yourself, Van. Who would think their own father was capable of something like that? I'm still shocked. It doesn't seem like the man I met at all. He was always very proud of you. He was there when you won gold." She quickly bit her lip, afraid Van would ask how she knew that, but he was deep into his own introspections.

"When my achievements reflected well on him, yes, he was proud." He retook his seat next to her. His profile was angular and his voice crisp. "But he had a petty, superficial side. I saw it when my equipment line started doing well. Growing up, Mom took credit for my genes and the quality of my training, but Dad paid for my coaching and travel. It all went through the company as a marketing expense, but he liked to say I wouldn't have been able to develop as an athlete without him which..." He wobbled his head as he debated that. "It's not *un*true, but it's not the whole truth." He took a deep drink of his beer.

Van's father had been an arrogant sort, but Becca had always taken his little asides about all that he had done for Van as a knock against herself and whatever contribution she thought *she* was making to Van's success.

"I would have had a much harder time rising to such an elite level if I hadn't had his backing in my early years," Van admitted. "But Mom had a lot of connections that were arguably more valuable. Once I got enough sponsorship to pay for my own training, Dad had fewer bragging rights to my accomplishments. Things got really contentious between us a year or so before I met you. We kept it quiet, but there was a claim from a local band over a swath of land my great-grandparents had bought when they first moved up here from Vancouver. It was a gray area as to whether their purchase was legal in the first place. I mean, if we're talking about treaties and lack thereof, it wasn't legal at *all*, but it was on the company books as an asset. The band called it out as improper seizure. Dad wanted to fight it all the way to the Supreme Court to keep it. He was trying to gather investors so he could develop the property to pay the legal fees. I voted with Mom and Paisley to give it back and eat the loss. It was the right thing to do, but Dad took it very personally that I didn't side with him."

"Is that why the company was struggling? Because you gave up that land?"

"Yes, but we had a plan to recover and it seemed to be working. All the right things were being said at the board meetings, anyway. Dad and I seemed to move past the worst of his resentment, but that's why I should have paid attention when he kept assuming I would bring my capital with me when I joined the company."

"Maybe you would have, if he'd been honest about why he needed it."

"Not likely," he said flatly. "I didn't want to work with him. I already knew we would be at odds. I wanted to build affordable housing and he was all about maximizing profit, driving down wages, cutting corners. Once we clashed over the land claim, I knew we would never be able to work together. I told him that, but he figured I would come around. He finally started to believe me when you and I bought this house and it wasn't one of his."

Becca bit her lip. She had found this house kind of by accident. She had heard through the grapevine that the builder was running out of money. It had been very whirlwind. She and Van had come out for a look and happened on the owner as he was installing a gutter. They made an offer on the spot, he accepted it. A few weeks later, they were finishing the house to their own tastes.

Van had given Becca free rein to turn it into their dream home. She had made the bulk of decisions and paid for incidentals as it was completed. Since she hadn't been working, this had been her full-time job, chasing contractors and looking at swatches and shopping for furniture, but she still felt wrong laying any claim to it. Now another layer of remorse was upon her. She hadn't realized this house had caused such a big rift between Van and his father, one that had led to Jackson doing something truly atrocious.

"You didn't have to buy it, Van. Not if it was such a bone of contention between you and your father."

"I wanted to. It's a great house, a perfect location. Frankly, I loved that Dad didn't have a single fingerprint on it. Maybe I'm as petty as he is," he muttered into his mug. "But I was tired of my parents using me as a weapon against each other. Or being the trophy they fought over. Marrying you, buying this house… It wasn't rebellion. It was growing up. I was becoming my own person. That felt good. I refuse to apologize for it."

"But he felt threatened by that? By your buying a house without his input?" By *her*? How laughable, but it did explain why his father had been so disinclined to like her.

"Was he peeved that I bought a house in which he made no money on the transaction? Absolutely. And it's not as if I made any effort to reassure him." His thumb moved restlessly on the handle of his mug. "When you flew home to Sydney, I pulled the pin. I told him I'd be staying with you there after the games, if that's where you needed to be. He was furious. He said he wanted to retire and I was a selfish ingrate who went back on his promises."

She swallowed a sickly lump from her throat. "I didn't know you told him that before you left."

"Don't," he dismissed gruffly. "You don't bear any responsibility for his actions, Becca. I wish I could blame someone else, but if anyone else is to blame, it's me. I told him those were assumptions on his part, not promises on mine. B&D has always had succession plans in place, things the board can do if something happens to the CEO. I said if he wanted to retire without my taking over, there were options and he should exercise them. I never imagined he would watch me win, look me straight in the eye when he shook my hand, then fly home early to take the money and run."

It was a breath-catching shock to hear it stated so flatly. "I can't fathom what a blow it was when you heard. I'm so sorry."

"Not your fault," he assured her. "And it was hard for a while, getting past the shock, taking on so much responsibility. I knew how to run a company, but Van Scott Equipment started very small and I handpicked all my leadership. Designing a pair of skis and approving a marketing strategy did not prepare me to plan and execute a housing project. We had dozens in different stages of completion across the country. Investors wanted to cash out. If only Mom and Paisley had been affected, I would have dusted off my hands and found a way to get them back on their feet. That wasn't an option, so I threw my own money in to cool tempers and got down to work."

"*And* you made the fitness app. I've seen it."

"I actually put Paisley on the team and it's done surprisingly well. It boosts equipment sales, too. And I don't mind working at B&D because I'm in charge.

I can steer us toward the projects I think are valuable in ways beyond financial—passive design, minimal environmental impact, a mix of affordable and up-scale housing. Our teams are winning awards. We're getting tons of contracts."

"That's great."

"It is. That's why it's so strange that you've cho-sen *now* to turn up again."

"What do you mean?" Her blood seemed to still in her veins.

"This whole thing left deep scars, Becca. I'm not nearly so trusting as I used to be. People you're sup-posed to be able to believe in—your father, your wife—can turn on you." He swiveled his head to send her a look that slammed hard into her own. "I mean it this time. I want to know why you're here."

The antagonism in his voice was such a baffling shift, she took a moment to absorb it.

"You think I want to *turn* on you? How? Steal from you the way your father did?"

"I don't know. You tell me."

Every time she had a glimmer of thinking maybe they had something worth saving, she came smack up against what a lost cause they really were.

"I want my locket." She touched her empty throat where the small pendant had sat in the early days of their relationship. "I used to wear it before we mar-ried. It's a small gold heart—"

"I know which one you're talking about, but do

you really expect me to believe that? It's worth less than a bus ticket from Vancouver, nowhere near a plane ticket from Sydney."

So disparaging. She understood why he was embittered, she did, but she wasn't his father. Did he realize that? Tears came into her eyes.

"No. I don't expect you to believe me," she said with a pang of despair. "I completely understand that things like sentimentality for a parent would be foreign to you, especially now." She gave a couple of rapid blinks to clear her vision. "But my mother gave it to me and Wanda has hers. I'm not leaving until I find mine."

She shoved herself off her stool and hurried up the stairs.

CHAPTER EIGHT

"Becca."

The timer on the oven sounded as Van tried to call her back. *Damn it.*

He rose to check the cake, then had to find and wash an empty wine bottle to set the thing to cool upside down on the neck. What a ridiculous procedure, but he'd be damned if he would burn or ruin it.

I'm making you a cake, aren't I?

It was nostalgia, Van. You think we're the first couple to have one for the road?

He'd been stung by that, still awash in postorgasmic chemicals and wanting to keep that train rolling. But she didn't think they should put much stock into it.

Any leftover tenderness from their passionate clash had completely faded as he revisited his father's treachery. He'd almost forgotten the part Becca had played in all of that. Not that she'd done it on purpose, but his father had seen Van's decision to stay in Sydney as choosing Becca over plans that had been in place for at least a decade.

That final altercation had been a lot worse than Van had revealed to Becca. Even though he had been determined to do his own thing and genuinely didn't want to work with his father, his father's accusations had landed hard. Van had wondered if he was more like the rest of his family than he wanted to be, using people when they were convenient, walking away from a commitment when it no longer suited him.

In his mind, he'd been sticking by the vows he'd made to Becca—only to have her tell him their marriage was over. That had been enough for him to pigeonhole her under "people who screwed me over" and expect her to do it again.

She'd been injured by his accusation, though. He'd watched her big brown eyes dim with startled hurt. The fact was, Becca was exactly sentimental enough to come all this way for a modest locket. That earnest softness in her was the reason he'd been drawn to marry her. She wasn't like most of the people who surrounded him, all pushing and shoving for higher returns and status symbols and whatever else they thought he could give them.

Was the locket her only reason for being here? He just didn't know. As he'd been thrust back into the swamp on the heels of his father's departure, he'd resented Becca for leaving him to navigate that alone. For not having her calm warmth to come home to. It wasn't like her. He'd grown used to her being there for him.

He closed his eyes in a wince, recognizing his father's selfishness in that thought. Worse, Van had been busy when he returned. So freaking buried under work, traveling, taking calls at all hours... He would have fallen into the pattern they had already established. Instead of telling her he had to train, he would have said he had to work. Despite his best claims in Sydney, nothing would have changed for her.

I was alone here so often, I forgot I was married.

She was divorcing him because she hadn't had a husband in the first place. That was the undeniable truth. If she had wanted his money, she could have been spending it all this time, but she hadn't.

No, she had booked her trip back here around her friend's schedule—which was exactly like her to accommodate someone else. It made perfect sense that she would retrieve something that held deep meaning for her while she was here.

Ah, hell. He had some explaining to do about that locket himself.

Silently cussing himself out, Van left the kitchen and detoured into the den where his laptop lived on his desk. His gold medals were locked in the safe behind an enlarged glossy photo of him catching air during a long-ago race in Switzerland.

As he retrieved the small envelope, he winced

again at how creased and dingy it had become. He almost reached into a drawer for a new one, but Becca wouldn't care about the envelope. She wanted the contents and… Damn, damn, damn.

He made his way up to the bedroom where Becca was in the closet, going through all the pockets on an assortment of handbags. A half dozen of them were scattered on the floor.

"Here," he said, offering the envelope.

"You found it?" She hurried out of the closet. "Where was it?"

"In the safe."

"Why? It's not worth much, as you so bluntly pointed out."

The sharpness of her tone cut almost as deeply as her small whimper when she poured the necklace into her hand and realized the front of the heart was no longer attached to the back.

"It's broken." Her voice cracked as she sank onto the foot of the bed, shoulders sloping, corners of her mouth curving down.

He closed his eyes in remorse. When he pushed his hands into his pockets, a full year after he'd realized the front had broken off, his fingertips still searched for the tangled chain and the small nugget of the heart, as if he would still find it in the bottom corner, tangled with lint.

Becca pinched the chain and gave it a delicate shake, plucking in an attempt to loosen the knots.

"Why is it so tangled and beat up? Did it go through the washing machine?"

"No. I…" He scratched the back of his head. "I actually had it on me in Sydney. I forgot or I would have given it to you." That was true. His mind had been firmly shattered by her desire to end their marriage, then the news about his dad.

"Why did you bring it to Sydney?" She blinked her surprise at him.

"I grabbed it as I was leaving for the airport. It was on the hook by the bathroom window. I took it because…" He shrugged, trying to make light of what had actually become an important talisman during his two weeks of competing, especially when he realized she wasn't coming. "It was a mind game. I told myself I already had gold."

"Mmm. Manifest what you want by believing you already have it?" She smiled faintly. "I think it's only nine karats, but whatever works." She was putting a brave face on it, but he could see she was blue at having it returned to her in such bad shape.

He opened his mouth to explain that she was the gold he'd had, that he'd wanted her with him for every nanosecond of his races, but he didn't want to lay another guilt trip on her for not being there. The first one had sent her into hysterics.

It was also too revealing to admit how important it had been to him. He was as superstitious as the next athlete and had worn his share of playoff beards or whatever else might have kept him on a winning streak, but that didn't explain why he'd put the damned thing in his pocket every morning for months after their marriage was over, when he'd been so angry with her he should have been happy it snapped in half. Instead, he'd carried a crushing guilt, carefully tucking the pieces into that envelope until the creases had started to wear at the corners. He'd been seriously worried he would lose some part of it, so he'd put it in the safe.

"I've been meaning to take it to a jeweler to get it fixed." He hadn't wanted to give it up. Not even for a few days. At least while it was in his safe, he knew it *was* safe.

"This is why I limit my expectations," she said with a tone that was supposed to be ironic but held an underlying despair. She tried to line up the front of the heart with the back. "All I wanted was to put it on and even that's beyond my reach."

Self-reproach nearly buried him. The locket would have been fine if he'd left it alone, and he had to wonder if it was a metaphor for them. *They* might have been better off if he'd left her alone. He couldn't blame her if she thought that.

She carefully poured it back into the envelope, then stood to tuck it in the front pocket of her jeans. "Thanks. I feel better now that I know where it is. Sorry about the mess. I'll clean it up."

She moved into the closet and started gathering

handbags off the floor, putting them on the shelves, not throwing anything into the suitcase. The box with her glasses and the beads had made its way into the case along with some of Paisley's branded yoga wear and a Van Scott hoodie, but little else.

"I should have brought the rest of the jewelry from the safe. I'll get it." He turned.

"Don't bother. Give it to Paisley or your mom." She was rehanging a quilted parka, fixing the pockets she'd turned inside out. "Save it for Flora."

"I bought it for *you*, Becca. Don't you like any of it?"

"I love every single piece." She looked up with surprise. "But it seems rude to keep it. I brought my rings to give back to you, too. They're in my purse. I'll get them as soon as I finish cleaning up."

"What the hell am I supposed to do with your wedding rings?" His voice grew loud enough that she fell back a step.

"What am *I* supposed to do with them?" she asked quietly, crossing her arms. "I'm not going to walk around wearing wedding rings when I'm divorced."

"Sell them and use the money for school. Put a down payment on a place to live." He flung a hand in different directions, not caring how she spent it so long as he knew she was building some security for herself. "I want you to have what you need, Becca."

"Van." She blew a breath out to the ceiling. "If I take the jewelry and sell it, I might as well have asked you for the cash four years ago. I don't go anywhere that requires me to dress up in evening gowns and diamond earrings, so I don't need any of this." She waved at the garment bags hanging next to his suits. "When I say you and I were always too different, this is what I mean. You do this. I don't."

"You don't expect any hospital fundraisers in your future, once you're working in that industry?" A searing blaze of jealousy with a flame of green burning in its center swept up, nearly burning him alive. "Doctors are even more devoted to their jobs than I was to skiing, you know."

"That's kind of a mixed message. Should I plan for a gala or not? How about I'll take one just in case?" She peeked into an open garment bag and plucked out purple silk. "I've always been sad that I never got to wear this one." She came out to drop a pair of silver shoes into the suitcase and shook out the gown, trying to work out how to fold it. "Happy?"

"Is that the dress you were going to wear to the reception Mom was planning if I won?"

"*When* you won," Becca corrected mockingly because his mother had trained all of them to play those mind games of assuming a wanted outcome had already happened. Cheryl had booked a hotel ballroom, had the invitations printed and pressed Becca to have something suitable to wear long before they'd known Becca would be in Sydney and unable to attend. "What happened with that party? Did you have it?"

"No," he said flatly. "Mom canceled—" very begrudgingly "—when I told her I wouldn't come back for it regardless of whether I won or not." She had tried to resurrect it when he did return, not seeing that the issues with Van's father would have made such a party tasteless in the extreme.

Becca turned to the mirror and held the dress against herself, cocking her head to admire it. "Maybe I'll call up Mum's oncologist, see if he has any events coming up."

"Don't wear it for someone else. *That's* rude."

"He's sixty and his husband organizes casino nights for charities," she said in a pithy tone. "Plus, women wear clothes to please themselves, not the male gaze." She looked back at her reflection. "And to feel superior to other women. Obviously."

"Obviously," he agreed drily.

"But that's part of pleasing ourselves." She hugged it to her waist. "Are you really not going to let me take it? I'm genuinely sad I never got to wear it."

He was feeling cheated he would never see her in it. "Wear it now." *Wear it for me.*

"Don't be silly. Swan around the house for an hour trying not to spill wine on it?"

"Why not? I won. We never celebrated that. And

it's New Year's Eve. I'll put on a suit. One last date."
His heart pinched as he said it.

"Last meal, more like," she said out of the side
of her mouth.

He snorted so he wouldn't give in to other more
conflicted emotions. It bothered him that the heart
was going home with her and little else.

*When I say you and I were always too different,
this is what I mean.*

"I can't cook in this." She frowned.

"I said I'll cook. I've already showered. I only
need to change. You, on the other hand, will need at
least an hour to go through whatever makeup Paisley left in the spare bedroom before you even start
getting ready."

Becca made a noise of offense. "*That's* rude. I
can be ready in ten minutes when necessary." She
wrinkled her nose with indecision. "But I was feeling sooky that I wouldn't get my New Year's Eve
with Courtney. Should we? It would end things on
a good note."

A heavy weight settled inside his chest. He didn't
think there was such a thing as ending a marriage
on a "good" note, but this would beat the hell out of
that death walk he'd made back to his hotel room
in Sydney.

"Might as well go out with a bang."

"Oh, I'm pretty sure we already did that." She
winked and sashayed down the hall.

* * *

Becca hadn't been on a date since she'd returned to Australia. She hadn't had time and hadn't been interested in more than catching up over coffee with a few girlfriends. Dating men had felt like something that should wait until she was divorced anyway.

Even back when she'd lived here with Van, proper dates had been few and far between. They would have dinner out sometimes, but she had often preferred to cook so she could have him to herself, otherwise they invariably ran into someone he knew and any sense of intimacy would be lost. Between his parents and Paisley and his own company, they'd attended family gatherings and charity dinners and product launches that weren't about spending time together as a couple, more like showing up and showing off as one.

Much as those events had made her feel out of her depth, she had liked how popular she felt when she was out with him. It had been an incredible confidence booster that people sought them out. They wanted to talk to Van because he was Van. They liked to talk to her because people at a party were no different from people at a bar. They wanted to talk about themselves and Becca always encouraged them. She was often told that she was charming and "a great listener" when really, she just preferred not to talk about herself and made self-deprecating jokes when she did.

Van had always been very attentive when they were out, which had added to the pleasure of an evening. He stayed near enough to touch her back or hold her hand, fetched a drink and exchanged little asides.

That guy was married to my mom for nine days.

That woman plays bass in the band on that singing show you like. Maybe she can introduce you to that singer you have a crush on.

She smiled to herself as she recalled those fun times, teasing each other and doing good work here and there, raising money for different causes like climate change and Lyme disease. She had actually enjoyed those sorts of functions, feeling like she was making an important contribution when she sat on a phone bank or sold raffle tickets.

She had deliberately blocked out the fact that when things had been good, they'd been really good. If she had allowed herself to remember that, she would have stayed blind to all that was wrong because it had only been as she got back to Sydney, and all the underpinnings of her hope and happiness in her marriage had begun snapping, that she'd lost faith in him and them.

She grew introspective as she showered and worked with a few items from Paisley's collection, adding them to the mascara and lip balm in her own bag.

It occurred to her that this was exactly how she had behaved back then, allowing her hurts to be glossed over by the bright life Van offered, never confronting them. In one way she was touched that he'd carried her necklace with him when he raced, but she hadn't let herself be angry that he'd trashed it. Her first thought had been that it was her fault for leaving it here. Rather than say, "You should have taken better care of it," she had tucked it away to fix it herself and was letting herself be distracted by playing dress-up.

The truth was, she had leaped at the chance to relive a time when he had admired and wanted her. She was trying to impress him and maybe she wanted him to feel at least a little of this loss that was sitting inside her for a marriage that never should have happened in the first place.

"Hey, Bec?" his voice called through the bathroom door. "You almost ready? I'm putting the steaks on."

Becca had never worn a lot of makeup even when Van's credit card meant she could afford the fancy stuff. Once she was married, however, she had had a woman at a salon give her some tips on applying everything properly. She had her cheekbones accentuated and her eyes wide and long-lashed as a baby fawn. Her hair had always liked the water here and had come out like the sassy end of a shampoo ad. She had already glossed her lips and was wearing a pair of earrings with colorful, dangling crystals and an armband with similar beads hanging off it.

"Yes, go ahead," she called back. "I'll be down in a sec." She was out of time. He liked his steak rare.

She didn't bother searching out an adhesive bra. Van had seen what she had a couple of hours ago and this halter bodice would be ruined if she had bra straps showing. When she had had this gown made, she had fallen in love with its wide satin waistline and skirt that fell in a graceful drape. It swept back from a thigh-high slit as she walked. Once she stepped into the sinfully sexy shoes, she almost looked tall and lithe.

Nerves attacked as she gripped the stair rail with a damp palm and descended to the living room.

Van had everything under control. He'd switched the music so it played a lulling melody beneath the sizzle of the steak. The table was set with a pair of embroidered linen place mats. He'd found the good silver and cloth napkins and even lit a candle. He must have grabbed the wine from the bedroom while she was in the shower because it was on the table with fresh glasses.

He had changed into his tuxedo, the impossibly handsome wretch. He knew she couldn't resist a pleated shirt and a bow tie. He wore only the vest, no jacket, and she would have teased him about dressing like a maître d', but they both knew he only had to shoot his cuffs and said, "Scott. Van Scott," and he could have her right there on the dining room table.

He flipped the steak with a pair of tongs, cut the

gas and fan, yelling over his shoulder, "Becca! I'm plating—"

"I'm right here."

He swore and swung around. His head went back as if he'd been struck. He raked his gaze down and up, swore again and let his gaze take another long sip, this time more slowly.

She pressed her lips and planted her hand on her hip, hitched her weight to one side so her thigh poked from the slit. With a preening flick, her hair went behind her shoulder.

"Really?" she asked to the ceiling. "You knew I was here."

"I forgot exactly how superior you are to other women."

She sputtered a laugh. "Oh, please. I'm easy, but I'm not that easy." She walked toward the island, blushing with pleasure at his silly compliment and trying to dispel it. "Do you need help?"

"I got it." He plated the food and prepared to carry it to the table, nodding for her to walk ahead of him.

She didn't need to glance over her shoulder to know his gaze was sliding all over her backless gown and swaying hips. She felt it as a delicious shiver down her naked spine.

She glanced back anyway, and his brows went up, unapologetic, as she dipped her chin in a scolding *caught you*.

It was a cheeky exchange that warmed her

through, but also pushed her onto the seesaw of wishing and wanting and fearing a hard bump was coming.

He set the plates, saying ruefully, "You're not easy. I thought you were, but you're not."

"We're ignoring what happened downstairs?" It was supposed to be a throwaway joke at her own expense. She was certainly trying to ignore it, but when she met his gaze her shell of self-deprecation fell away and she was all raw nerve and exposed emotions. Her throat stung all the way down to between her breasts.

The heat and humor in his gaze banked. "In that way, we're both pretty damned easy," he said solemnly and held her chair, then poured their glasses before seating himself.

It struck her that they were trying to be silly and fun and make the most of a situation the way they would have while they were married, but those tactics of falling back on lust and playful avoidance no longer worked. They had grown up too much.

"This looks very nice," she noted. He had added the last of the shrimp to the pasta along with sun-dried tomatoes and artichoke hearts. Broccoli and carrots and red bell pepper burst with color beside the well-peppered steak. "Thank you."

"Go big or—" He stopped himself.

"And then go home?" she suggested. She gave a chagrined sigh as they began to eat. "I didn't find you easy, either. Maybe it was this." She waved at the house and the meal and what she wore. "I was always waiting for you to realize I didn't belong here. I was waiting for you to get tired of me. Waiting for you to *be* here," she acknowledged with a twist of her lips.

"I thought you wanted to be here." His brows came together in an absent frown. "You came to Canada and married me so you could stay. You found the house and made it ours. I thought this *was* our home, Becca. Where did I go wrong that you didn't see it that way?"

"It wasn't you." She twirled noodles onto her fork, but didn't eat them.

Her temptation was to make some remark, deflect, steer the conversation away from herself. Who even cared what she had to say anyway? That's why she didn't talk about herself. She didn't feel interesting and griping never changed anything.

But he was waiting so patiently to hear where *he* had gone wrong.

Chest aching, she tried to explain.

"You're right that I limit myself. That I don't have a lot of self-confidence. Part of it was growing up in a rough area and having—not a bad reputation, but not a good one." She had never wanted him to know this. That's why she hadn't told him. "School was not a happy time for me. I developed early so that made girls jealous and boys a nuisance. I was teased because I scrubbed toilets at the petrol station and had

caught lice once. I wanted to train for a 'real job.'"
She air quoted. "But even my teachers didn't think
I had much potential. One said it was a lucky thing I
was built to sell cars since I didn't get good grades."

"A *teacher* said that? Give me his name," he said
in a voice so deadly it raised the hairs on her arms.
"He and I need to have a conversation."

"It was a woman," she said with a curl of her lip.
"I've since heard she's no longer allowed to teach,
but her comment stuck with me. It made the fact that
I would even think about coming here a bold move.
You've always traveled for races and training and va-
cation. It's no big deal to you to hop on a plane, but as
a family, we hardly went down to the beach. I didn't
tell them what I was planning. I saved up in secret
and applied for the visa thinking I wouldn't even be
selected, even though I knew heaps of people who
got them. I've always had this constant sense that *I*
don't get things that others do. Maybe that's why I
don't," she said with a small shrug of realization. "I
mean, if you can't imagine yourself winning a gold
medal, you don't even bother trying, right?"

She had never been so honest and he was listening
intently, not saying anything. Somehow that made
it harder to continue than if he'd told her not to feel
this way. It made her listen to herself and hear how
she had let her own insecurities weigh her down and
hold her back.

"Mum was like this, too. Maybe she taught me to

be this way by example. She really struggled after my birth father died. Her family hadn't approved of her living with him outside of marriage and refused to help her. They were teaching her a lesson, you know? That's what you get when you go against the grain."

Keep your head down, possum.

"Dad is kind of the same," she continued. "He likes a simple life and they lived in what they viewed as the natural order of things. They both worked, but he watched footie while she cooked his dinner. My grades weren't the best so when I said I wanted to try a year at uni, Dad said I didn't need to go there to find a husband. He thought I should take hairstyling or something that I could do between having kids." Her heart twisted as she repeated that.

"It's a real mystery why you didn't tell them you were planning to come to Canada."

"Right?" She cleared her throat, recalling with another pang, "Mum was so upset. 'What do you want to go there for?'" she repeated in her Mum's broad accent. "She knew I was trying to reinvent myself away from the life she'd given me. She took it as a criticism and rejection. For her, getting us settled with Dad was so much better than the life she had been able to give me that my wanting more than that was just me being greedy."

"You were doing exactly what young adults are supposed to do. You struck out on your own and tried to figure out who you were." He sat back, sipping his wine.

"I know, but I thought I would *show her*. I would become this amazing, successful person and she would realize I was right to come here, but four years in I hadn't achieved anything. I was still screamingly ordinary and had new mistakes dragging behind me like a broken tailpipe." She had bumbled between a half dozen service jobs and gotten herself dumped by a couple of second-rate men. She had made some new friends, but had still been sharing a bedroom and eating too many packets of instant ramen noodles. "I started to realize it wasn't the place. It was the person. That was demoralizing."

"Don't say that, Becca. No one has their act together at that age."

"You did," she said on a scoffing laugh. "You were winning your hundred-bazillionth race. You had always known exactly what you wanted and you were doing the work to get it. So when you looked at me…" She gulped, but the shards in her throat only sank into the space behind her breastbone. "It didn't make sense. You could have had anyone."

"I wanted *you*."

"I didn't see why you should, though." She opened her hands, pleading for him to understand. "I let us happen because I thought some of your drive and success would rub off on me. At the very least, I could tell Mum I had this famous boyfriend. *Husband.*"

"*That's* why you married me?" He set down his cutlery and sat back, expression frosting over.

"I married you because I loved you." Her voice shook as she said it, feeling as though she had inched out on a thin plank over a chasm. "But I knew you would never love me. How could you? I was boring and small and ordinary." Her eyes welled so she couldn't see him properly. She could feel his gaze drilling holes through her, though. She used her napkin to dab beneath them. "I didn't have grand ambitions or any hope of achieving them." That wasn't quite true. She had known exactly what she wanted. It hadn't seemed all that grand, either. In this modern age, it was almost regressive to aspire to make a baby, but even that very ordinary dream was beyond her reach. "Your family saw what a fraud I was. They knew I wasn't like the rest of you. I knew it was only a matter of time before you saw it, too."

She didn't have much appetite, but swirled a fresh bite of noodles onto her fork and ate it, tentatively glancing at him as she chewed, not sure what to make of his silence.

He wore a thunderous expression that turned her mouthful into sawdust. She quickly washed it down with a swallow of wine.

"Two people *like* me got married and would have killed each other if they hadn't divorced. One of them was so full of ambition and entitlement he destroyed the life he had supposedly built for me and my sister and his *grandchildren*. Adjust your vision of what great people look like, Becca." He shoved to his feet and walked away.

She swung her head to watch him cross into the living room. Beyond him, she caught her indistinct reflection in the blackened windows.

"I didn't ask you to be anything but who you are." He pivoted to confront her, voice booming up to the rafters of the loft. "If you had ended our marriage because you thought you deserved better, I could accept that. Instead, you thought you knew what I wanted." He jabbed at his chest. "And decided you weren't it. You don't know what I want, Becca."

"I did so!" She rose so quickly her chair skittered and almost tipped. She took a few agitated steps toward him, skirt brushing her legs, and waved her arm at the kitchen and the stairs and herself. "You wanted a Cinderella mouse who would cook and keep your bed warm, but also throw on a dress like this and talk nonsense to CEOs and their wives."

"Sure," he agreed, nodding. "And you were damned good at all of that. I also wanted someone who wanted the man, not the name on a pair of skis. I didn't even believe in love, let alone the kind that comes without conditions attached, but I almost believed that's what you offered me. I *wanted* to believe it."

A flaming arrow seemed to shoot across and land in her chest, stopping her breath.

"Then you cut me off the minute I retired." His hand sliced through the air. "I came home to my father's disaster and you... What? What did you tell your mom about me then? I guess I wasn't such a catch at that point. She probably congratulated you on having the sense to leave me behind."

"That wasn't what I said. I told her our marriage had just been for immigration." Becca hadn't been able to tell her mum why she'd defaulted on her marriage any more than she was able to admit it to Van. "I didn't want her to think badly of you."

"That's okay then, I guess?" He ran his hand down his face.

He was hurt. She could hear it. She stared at the floor with stinging eyes, hands folded before her, contrite and filled with sorrow and despair while all sorts of words gathered in her mouth like hard, oversize marbles.

I did love you, she wanted to insist. *You should have believed me.*

She had wanted the same thing, to be loved without condition. It had never seemed possible and it wasn't. Not if he thought love was an illusion. A manipulation tactic. How could she ever convince him otherwise, given his experience? She couldn't.

The clock in the corner, the one he called "my grandfather's clock" because the long case had belonged to his father's father, chimed eight times. They both stared at it until it silenced. Then there was only the sound of the guitar notes picked out beneath a ballad that bemoaned a time "when we were young."

"I don't want to fight," she murmured. "Can we…?" She motioned to the table.

They weren't fighting. They were doing what they should have done four years ago. Talking. *Really* talking.

It was uncomfortable as hell, which was why they had skirted it then.

Van needed a minute to gather his thoughts so he nodded jerkily and came to hold her chair. They both sat, but only picked at their food.

Had she loved him? He still didn't understand what that emotion was, only having received a version of it that had been loaded with obligation and guilt. His parents had said it to him when he had been very young, but he hadn't really heard it much after their divorce. When he had, love had seemed to be a quantifiable feeling, something they expected to receive from him in measures of greater amount than he gave the other. Paisley hadn't been much better, sneaking around with a lot of, "Thanks for covering for me. Love you, bro."

Love had never been the soft, reassuring, healing emotion the pop songs and rom-coms promised.

He supposed he felt something like that toward his niece and nephew. They showered him with affection for the small trade of his giving them his attention. He easily imagined risking his own life to save theirs, but that was the same primitive emotion any man felt for his tribe. He felt the same thing toward his mother and sister and yes, toward Becca. She'd been his mate, so he wanted to protect her and provide for her even now.

There'd been other layers between them, too. Passion and sexual possessiveness and friendship, but he'd kept a wall up. They both had.

For all his bravado tonight, saying that they ought to get out whatever they'd held back in the past, he wasn't sure there was value in tearing down that wall. They would part again in a few hours, this time for good. Did they want to do that with their souls intact? Or in tatters?

He definitely didn't want to crack the subtle self-assurance Becca had gained. She still had a certain vulnerability in her shadowed expression, but she was more mature and confident than four years ago. She had a sense of purpose. An aspiration that put a spark of excitement in her voice and face.

It put a fiery streak of knowledge behind his sternum that she wanted things beyond their marriage and him. She always had and he'd refused to see it.

"You must have felt like this, a bottle in a cellar." He picked up his glass and tilted the ruby liquid in its bowl. "I stuck you in this house and expected you to be here whenever I returned." He hated coming into an empty house. That was the real reason he was selling it.

"Sometimes," she murmured, lashes flickering.

"In my defense, I dreamed of having empty days with no one clamoring for my time or attention, no one correcting my form or counting my reps. If I couldn't have that myself, it seemed like the next best thing to give it to you. I shouldn't have assumed you'd want that. I should have asked you what you wanted and supported you while you achieved it."

Her mouth wobbled. She set down her fork and pressed her hands into her lap. Her eyes were misting up again and he couldn't take it. It made his lungs burn.

"If you're not going to eat, let's dance." He needed to hold her, just hold her and stem what felt like a deadly bleed in his chest.

Helpless bewilderment flitted across her expression and she nodded-shrugged, allowing him to help her stand.

They moved to the area rug that sat beneath the two sofas, the very space he'd stood when he had railed at her a few minutes ago. He kneed the coffee table out of the way and they shuffled close in the small space. It wasn't dancing. It was an excuse to hold each other because they'd always been better at physical communication than verbal.

He wrapped one arm around her waist and drew her in. Her arm went under his and her hand flattened against his shoulder blade. He held her free hand against his chest and after a few offbeat steps, she sighed and let her head rest in the hollow of his shoulder.

His thumb traced the spot where her backless gown exposed her spine and that's all it was for two whole songs, them swaying in place while they held each other. Everything within him settled for the first time in eons.

Then she tilted her face up and pressed her lips to his throat. Her breath warmed his neck as she asked, "Do you want to go upstairs?"

Which was when he realized he was hard. She must have felt it against her stomach and his brain was too fogged with arousal to notice anything beyond how good he felt holding her again.

"Yes," he rasped, distantly thinking he ought to be more rational. Think this through.

She stepped back and her nipples were peaked against the front of her dress. Hell, yes, he'd known she was braless, but it was an erotic sight all the same. Her eyelids were heavy, her bottom lip caught in her teeth. She picked up her skirt, turning to walk away in that seductive swagger that extremely high heels gave a woman.

His heart thudded in time with every step. He had enough awareness to detour across and blow out the candle before he followed her up the stairs. A voice in his head warned him that making love again would fix absolutely nothing, but who the hell cared? They'd already crossed this line. There was no making it worse.

Was there?

She was removing the armband from above her elbow when he entered the bedroom. He didn't let her take off anything else, stepping close behind her to sweep her hair to the front of one shoulder so he could press a kiss to the side of her neck.

Her small shudder and gasp were music. Heavenly. Earlier, he'd fallen on her like a man finding a mirage in a desert. He had plunged into the relief of being with her.

Not this time. This was an all-you-can-eat banquet and he intended to sample and taste every delectable inch of her. He brought her hand up to kiss the back of her knuckles and nuzzled along her forearm, dabbing his tongue into the crook of her elbow, smiling when her breath hitched again.

As her arm bonelessly sagged backward to drape behind his neck and she arched her breast beneath his lowered gaze, he smiled against the point of her shoulder and said, "Slowly this time. We have all night."

Only tonight. The knowledge weighted each touch with deep significance. This had to be sweet and perfect. Memorable. It would have to sustain him for the rest of his life.

"Becca." He breathed against her ear and swirled his tongue against the whorls, closing his eyes when she pressed her ass into his groin and released a helpless whimper.

How had he survived without the pliant globe of her breast in his hand? The taste of her skin when he scraped his teeth against the tendon down the side and kissed the love bite he'd left there earlier? Or the thrill it gave him to feel her head loll and her body sway into his as she grew weak?

It seemed impossible that she had bottled all this passion, not sharing it with anyone else. He was almost angry at her for denying herself. If she hadn't wanted anyone else, why hadn't she come to him?

He hadn't gone to her, either. A thousand tangled assumptions and threads of pride had been in his way.

Now he wanted nothing between them. He used one hand to open the button on the collar of her dress while kissing her flexing spine. The front fell forward over his hand where he still massaged her breasts. He moved his hand and now he cupped warm, bare skin. Her nipple poked into his palm and he groaned against her back, kissing his way down.

She was writhing, trying to turn, but he didn't let her. He sank to his knees and released the zip at the base of her spine, setting a kiss on her tailbone. The dress fell away and a midnight-blue thong framed the tops of her round cheeks. He groaned again and lightly bit each one.

"Van. I can't stand." Her hand was scrabbling backward for his shoulder, her legs wobbling.

He steadied her, then let her turn, staying on his knees while he shed his vest and left it on the floor. Heels. He was as helpless as any man to their sex appeal. He ate up the sight of her round hips and juicy thighs. Her stomach pulled in with tension and her breasts were lush and round and topped by those pretty nipples that made his mouth water with wanting the feel of them against his tongue.

"What's wrong?" Her voice was hazed with lust, her smile witchy as she tugged his bow tie loose. "You can't stand, either?"

"Hell of a view from here," he managed to say, caressing her ankles and calves and knees and thighs. When he got to the slash of midnight blue, he drew it off one hip, rose on his knees and kissed the soft spot beneath her iliac crest.

"Take off your clothes," she urged, fingers running along his collar, searching for buttons.

"In a minute," he murmured, wrapping his arm around her hips as he drew her thong down. He kissed across her stomach and blew softly against the fine hairs that covered her mound.

She shook in his hold, hands spearing into his hair.

"Step," he coaxed as he reached her shoe and drew the silk off and away.

This, now. His hand wasn't quite steady as he caressed back up her leg, finding the inside of her thigh and urging her to open her legs a little more.

"The shoes make you just the right height." He'd been too wild with need earlier, aching to be inside her. This time he indulged himself, losing himself in the taste of her, the way she quaked and moaned and clutched at him. The way she sobbed his name and finally shattered, crumpling in the aftermath so he had to pick her up and carry her to the bed.

He took off her shoes, liking that she was too weak to do anything but watch him, stomach still quivering as she tried to catch her breath.

He threw off his clothes, then started to pick up her leg, intent on throwing it over his shoulder as he said, "Let's do that again."

"No." She stopped him with that low, lust-soaked voice. "Me first." She sat up and motioned him to stand before her.

By the time Van said a guttural, "Turn around," they were both mindless, stripped down to pure sensation.

Becca had caressed him with her mouth until he insisted she stop. He had pressed her back onto the mattress again and slid his arms beneath her thighs and did it to her until she was arching and pulsating and calling his name.

It was only the beginning. His hands and mouth went everywhere. His body surged into hers and he drove her over the edge, then he pulled her atop him where she relaxed with him hard and throbbing deep inside her.

She luxuriated in his petting and kisses and lazy thrusts until need drove her to sit up on her knees and ride him. Perspiration broke out on her body and the excited flush of orgasm followed. She was sure there was nothing left in her, but now he was pulling pillows under her stomach and covering her. He slipped into her with exquisite ownership and tangled his hand in her hair while he whispered filthy, sexy, wicked things.

"I can't get enough of you when you're like this. You're so hot, so incredible. Tell me how hard you can take it." He started out slow, teasing her senses awake again until she was completely his, all inhibitions gone.

She groaned her encouragement and held herself still for his powerful thrusts. Each one sent cataclysmic sensations through her. "Van. Van!"

"Come with me." His fingers bit into her hips and her whole body was one live nerve. "I need you with me, Becca. Come now. *Now.*"

Ecstasy struck like a meteor, demolishing her hold on reality. They exploded and dissolved.

CHAPTER NINE

"ARE YOU OKAY?"

Van's question pulled Becca from her coma-like doze.

No. She was devastated that this was the last time she would feel this way. The last time his naked body would be half sprawled on hers, his thigh threatening to give her a dead leg, his voice a quiet rumble against her temple, his hand loosely cupping on her breast.

"I should have limbered up. I'll be sore tomorrow," she prevaricated, blinking her eyes open long enough to note they hadn't even turned the lights off. How debauched of them.

"Sauna's on," he reminded.

His breath was causing her hair to tickle her brow, but she was too weak to lift her arm and rub away the itch.

"Will you carry me out there?"

"I was going to ask you that."

She didn't want to move, but the sauna was a great place for making like a lizard. Somehow, they gathered their strength, put on robes and made the short trek through the falling snow.

Becca left her robe in the change room and walked naked into the sauna, where she spread two towels on the cedar benches. She took the lower one and released a luxurious exhale as the hard warmth of the wood radiated into her back.

Van came in a moment later with a bucket of snowballs. He threw two onto the hot rocks, releasing sizzles and puffs of steam. He left the bucket by her feet and stepped over her to take the top bench, setting his head on the end by her feet so he could reach the bucket and throw more snow on the fire.

Becca sniffed. "Sage?"

"Whatever was out there," he said of the essential oils that were kept on a shelf in the changing area. "I set the timer so we don't fall asleep and cook to death."

"Worse ways to go."

"S'pose." He dropped his hand off the edge of his bench. His fingertips tapped her shin.

She obeyed his silent request and crooked her knee so he could rest his hand there and trace circles against her skin, the way he always had.

It was easy and familiar and perfect. She could have wept.

She was going to have to tell him. She knew she

was, but they'd come all this way to such lovely accord. Her brain was going so far as to wonder if she could take a similar course in lab technology here in Canada even though Van had made no mention whatsoever of wanting anything but the divorce they'd agreed to.

"It matters, Bec. It shouldn't, but it docs."

"What?" She blinked her eyes open to the orange glow of soft recessed lights that lined the ceiling.

"Mom and Dad cheated on each other. On anyone they ever made commitments to. If Mom has been faithful to Werner, that's a first. And Paisley..." He squeezed her knee. "I get why you kept her affair a secret. It would have been more drama than I was up for at the time, but I never wanted to be like them. I thought I'd lose my mind with sexual frustration sometimes, but we were still married and I couldn't cross that line. I didn't expect you to go without, though. I wouldn't have thought less of you if you had, but it means a lot to me that you didn't."

"You're taking my word for it that I haven't been with anyone?"

"Shouldn't I?"

"Yes. But you did accuse me of coming here to steal from you."

A pause, then, "Yeah, I did."

He didn't say anything after that, but he hadn't fallen asleep. His thumb was rubbing her kneecap as though he would wear a groove into it.

After a long time, he admitted quietly, "I wanted to see you. I wouldn't have cared about anything you took, not really. It would have reaffirmed some of my most cynical beliefs about human nature, but the settlement you asked for is a joke. You should get more. Take the jewelry. Take whatever you want. But if you had refused to see me, I would have felt robbed."

He still expected them to divorce, then. She blamed the burn in her lungs on the hot air of the sauna.

"I don't want anything else," she assured him, voice husky as she lied, "This is enough."

Van was still pensive after the timer woke them. They showered together in the change room and he teased Becca, calling her "raccoon eyes" as he helped her wash the last of the makeup off her face. They kissed and lazily washed each other, and it was all as good as life could get, but a one-night, two-person sex orgy was *not* enough. Not for him.

That was the reality he was confronting as they went back inside and Becca went upstairs to dry her hair. He warmed his plate, which she had shoved in the fridge on the way to the sauna.

He was wolfing down what remained of his dinner, chasing it with wine, when she reappeared. She wore her robe, and her hair was still damp on the ends, but swept back in waves off her face. Her skin was glowing, her eyes sleepy and her mouth soft.

She was the most beautiful woman he'd ever seen, especially when she lifted a smug brow at him. "Worked up an appetite, did you?"

An old, familiar sensation hit him. He wasn't one to soul-search and identify his feelings and examine them and *sit* with them. He lived his life and dealt with whatever hit him in the face, but he hadn't felt this sweet, soft, elusive feeling since she had left so he chased it, trying to figure out what it was.

Amusement? It was a desire to laugh, yes. Nostalgia? Maybe that's all this bizarre night was, but this was a shade of both without being either... Hell, was it happiness? He usually associated that with the triumph of winning or the base contentment of being physically comfortable. His male ego was damned satisfied right now so yeah, he was happy in that regard. Maybe it was just the feedback chemicals of great sex and a full stomach?

"Yours is still in the fridge. I'm trying to be a gentleman and leave it for you," he said as she took out an empty plate.

"Help yourself." She flipped the cake onto the plate.

"Becca, no," he said firmly. "You haven't eaten your vegetables." She had the worst eating habits, she really did. "I'll warm your dinner if you don't have the strength. *Then* you can have dessert." He rose to put her plate in the microwave.

She ignored him and cut a generous wedge of

cake, dropped it into a bowl. She opened the freezer to take out the mint chocolate chip ice cream.

"No. That is all sorts of sacrilege. I forbid it."

She threw a scoop onto her cake, sat down, dug her spoon into the concoction, and looked him straight in the eye as she closed her mouth over the first bite.

The feeling hit him again. Harder. He wanted to grab her and laugh with her, kiss her and roll his eyes and argue that she really ought to eat something decent all at the same time.

He usually only felt this light when he was flying down ten kilometers of empty slope on a spring day, powder spraying around him. The kind of day he loved best.

He wanted to stay in this moment forever. He wanted her to stay here. With him. Forever.

The sassy light in her eyes faded into something that caught in his heart and tugged him to move closer. He shuffled to stand beside her and cupped the back of her head, memorized the open, defenseless look on her face. He felt the yearning he read in her expression because it was expanding within him.

He started to lower his head, wanting to kiss those cold lips and taste mint and sugar and something intangible that he needed more than food or air or a spring day on…

His phone began to burble with an incoming video

chat. He brought his head up, breaking their eye contact as he glanced at it.

"Mom," he noted with a prickle of dismay as he recognized her photo. He dropped his hand from Becca's hair and stepped away. "She probably wants to say happy new year. They're in Mexico." He nodded at the clock, which showed it was ten past ten here. That meant it was after midnight there. "Do you mind?"

"No, of course. She'll wonder why you're not answering if you don't. Should I leave?"

"No." He unplugged his phone from the charger and accepted the call. "Hi, Mom."

Cheryl Brimley, still using her maiden name after more marriages than Van could count, wore a hotel robe and full makeup. She was removing her earrings.

"Happy new year," she said briskly.

"Happy new year. I thought you and Werner were going to a party. You left right after 'Auld Lang Syne'?"

"We had a fight." She looked to her left as she settled onto a chair with a painting of a seascape behind it. "He's about to become an old acquaintance I've forgotten."

"Mom." Van winced at how cold she was after six years of a relationship that had seemed to be good for her. "Don't talk like people are disposable."

"We want different things. It happens to the best

of us. *You*, according to your sister." She adjusted a cushion behind her back. "I called Paisley expecting to speak to both of you. She told me you drove back to Whistler because Rebecca was in town. She wants to take some things from the house before the divorce is finalized?"

"Becca is here," he said with a note of warning. *Say one thing, Mom. One. Thing.*

Becca was not here. She rose and went downstairs, leaving her bowl melting on the island.

Van watched her go while his mother's "Oh?" hung like a soap bubble on the air.

Maybe she was taking in the fact that he didn't flip the camera to allow the pair to greet each other. Maybe she was noting he also wore a robe.

"I suppose the hotels were booked," she said, dragging his attention back to her image on the screen.

"This is still Becca's house as much as mine. We got snowed in, had dinner and a sauna. It's all very civilized." She should take some notes.

His mother made a noncommittal noise and smoothed a brow. "I was concerned when Paisley said you had rushed off to meet her. Rebecca always seemed to distract you from more important things."

"Like what?" He was genuinely taken aback. "My *wife* was important to me. Maybe you enjoy failing at marriage. You must or you wouldn't keep doing it, but I hate it."

"Donovan," she scolded.

"No, Mom." He was glad Becca was out of earshot. "If you had put one fraction of support behind my marriage that you did behind my career as an athlete, I would still be married."

"Do *not* lay that at my door." Her back shot iron-straight. "*Or* lecture me on support. She didn't even show up to watch you compete in the most important—"

"Her mother was sick," he cut in starkly. "You didn't even call her to ask *why* she hadn't shown up. You had a thousand opportunities to make her feel like she was a part of this family and you squandered every single one. When I came home without her, you were glad. Why? Did you feel that threatened by her?" He hadn't meant to let all of this erupt out of him, but the tap was open and wouldn't close. "Did you feel like I was choosing her over you? Was that it?"

"Because you were planning to stay in Australia? For God's sake, Donovan, I didn't say one peep about that, did I? My focus was on getting you through the games without anything impacting your ability to perform. I did. *You're welcome.* You could have stayed in Sydney after that, and stayed married with my blessing. Your father was the one who took issue with your life choices and made off with the petty cash, if you recall. You came home to deal with that and I bear no responsibility for the fact your marriage didn't survive the distance. That is on you."

He bit back pointing out that his mother's not sharing her concerns with regards to said business had allowed his father to make off with the "petty cash" as she called it, but the harsh truth was Becca had already ended their marriage when that happened.

"As for whether I felt threatened by Rebecca, of course I did. Every mother feels her son's wife is taking him away from her. I didn't *dis*like her. I simply saw no point in growing attached if your marriage wasn't likely to last. I surmised correctly, didn't I? If you had had children, and I had foreseen a life-long relationship with her, I would have made more of an effort, the way I have with Gavin." She referred to Paisley's first husband, a man she still invited to barbecues and other events for the sake of her grandchildren.

"It's the part where you didn't expect my marriage to last that bothers me, Mom. Manifest the things you want, right? You know what's ironic. I thought you and Werner would stick. I wanted that for you. Happy new year."

"Donovan!" Her sharp use of his name made him hesitate in ending the call. "What are you saying?"

"I'm saying you should make an effort to work things out with Werner. Quit acting like marriage doesn't require give as well as take."

She touched her throat. "Is that what you're doing with Becca? Working things out?"

"I don't know, Mom. Not if I'm talking to you instead of her. I'll talk to you later." He ended the call.

If you had had children with her...

Becca heard most of Van's conversation. His voice and Cheryl's had drifted clearly down the stairs as Becca shakily poured out their watery drinks, set the glasses and blender to go upstairs into the dishwasher and ensured the bar was as pristine as it had been when she arrived. She also shamelessly pocketed their photo, deciding she wouldn't even ask him if she could have it. Somewhere there was a printed book of their honeymoon photos. She might steal that, too.

Van came downstairs looking shuttered and shut down the way his family always made him look.

Becca tensed, too aware of his, *I don't know, Mom. Not if I'm talking to you instead of her.*

"Too bad about her and Werner," she said, putting away the cue sticks.

"Yeah." He came to the other side of the table where he rolled a loose ball toward the far cushion and caught it when it came back to him. "I actually really like him, but that's Mom. She doesn't expect marriage to last so it doesn't bother her when it doesn't." Another dull thump as the ball silently rolled across the felt, bumped and came back. "And fine. I don't think anyone should stay married simply to say they did. Life is too short to be miserable, but it was drilled into me that you only fail if you give up. As long as you're trying, you still have a chance to get whatever it is you want."

He lifted his whiskey-gold eyes and pinned her in place with the mesmerizing fire that burned there.

She shoved her hands into the pockets of her robe where she curled them into tense fists, unconsciously bracing herself.

"I want *you*, Becca," he said simply.

Her heart skewed offside. She swallowed, both elated and devastated at once. She shook her head in refusal. It was hard. Harder even than when she'd done it in Sydney.

"Why not?" he asked grimly. "Look how good we are together."

"For a night," she said in a strangled voice. "This isn't real life, Van. I don't know if it ever was." She stared at the ghostly reflection of herself in the blackened window, exactly as she had always been here. Not solid, but translucent. More of a blurry version of herself than Becca, fully formed.

She longed to try again with him, she realized with a jolt that wasn't nearly as shocking as she wished it was. She could already see herself moving right back into that bedroom upstairs. Sharing their bed, cooking for them in the kitchen, walking

down to the water in the summer and watching the
snow fall in the winter.

It would be as simple as slipping into a warm bath
because—and this truth exploded with the force of
a sonic boom within her—she still loved him. God
knows she had tried to stop, but it wasn't something
that was dispelled by a good cry and a walk down
memory lane. It was the enduring kind that would
never lift off her heart because that's what her heart
was made of, now—love. For Van.

It shouldn't surprise her that he had taken com-
plete possession of that pulsing organ, not when she
had come all this way to retrieve a damned necklace
without asking him once if he'd seen it. He could
have mailed it to her if she had asked. Instead, as
the clock had ticked down on their marriage, she had
bought herself a plane ticket and come here for exactly this. One last hit of the drug called Van Scott.
One last chance to see…him.

One last chance for him to convince her to stay
and try again.

Why shouldn't she? Why go home and go to
school and build a fulfilling career in a city where
family who loved her resided, when she could give
up her own aspirations and live in the shadow of a
god again? Van always got what he wanted. If he
wanted *her*, who was she to deny him?

*Maybe you enjoy failing at marriage. You must
or you wouldn't keep doing it.*

With a small throb in her voice, she said, "No, Van. I won't stay here so you can tell yourself you didn't fail."

"I'm not asking you to stay. I'm telling you I'm coming with you to Australia."

"What? Why? How? *Why?*"

"I just told you why. To try again." Van sent the ball rolling into the far pocket and pushed his hands into his pockets. "We'll do what I wanted to do four years ago. We'll get a flat and live together and work things out from there. I'll have to come back at least once a quarter, but I already do a lot of work from home or wherever I happen to be traveling." He shrugged that off.

"Van." She rubbed between her brows. "Once I get my certification, it will be for working in Australia. I can't go to school there and come back here to work." She flicked her hand in vague directions.

"Well, you could. You would need to jump through some sort of bureaucracy hoops, but we'll cross that bridge if we decide to live here. Right now, the goal would be to pick up where we left off and see what sort of future we might have. Decide where we want our home to be."

"Why are you saying this? We agreed that our marriage was a mistake." She threw that at him like an accusation. Like he was being unreasonable.

"Why put off the inevitable? Let's make a clean break now while we can."

"Our marriage wasn't a mistake." He'd never been so sure of anything. "We made some, sure. Plenty. Both of us did. But we were learning how to be married, Bec. The good news is, we made all our mistakes up front. Now we know what not to do. It puts us in a stronger position moving forward."

"Yech." She folded her arms and hunched her shoulders, glaring at him. "That sounds like something you say to the board of directors at the strategy meeting."

He had lifted a few pat phrases, but, "It's still true. I didn't make our marriage a priority. I own that. I allowed my family to think you weren't important to me. You can bet they'll know in the future that nothing is more important to me than making our marriage work."

"Oh, like it's an engine that needs constant maintenance? That's very romantic, thanks." She was wearing her stubborn look, putting him on his back foot.

"I'm being honest with you, Becca. More honest than we were in the past. That's another area where I refuse to keep making mistakes." He gave her a stern look. "As for you, I get why you struggle to feel you deserve this kind of life. I'll try not to throw my money around if it makes you uncomfortable."

"And how will you do that?" she scoffed, still

hugging herself. "By saying you'll move around to the other side of the world and buy a flat in Sydney as if it's not some of the most expensive real estate on the planet?"

"Okay, yes." He was losing patience. "I will throw my money around if it means we can be together and comfortable. For God's sake, Becca. If we can afford nice stuff then I want to give it to you. That doesn't make me a bad person."

She was shaking her head again.

Frustration pushed him around the pool table toward her.

She stiffened and he halted. Sighed.

"Look at us. Neither of us has been with anyone else. We fell straight back into bed. *Twice*. Everything else between us clicks exactly the way it always has. We belong together. Why are you fighting that? *Be honest*."

"You're just trying to prove to your mother that you don't fail the way she does! Yes, I heard you say that!" she threw at him as he jerked his head back.

He flattened his lips. "You listened to all of it?"

"I couldn't help overhearing, could I? You were right there." She waved at the stairs where he'd stood near the top. He should have realized their voices were drifting down. "You want to stay married because it galls you to be like the rest of your family. Gosh, I can't wait to be that thing you work really hard on so you can be *right*."

"That's what you took from everything I said? Because I also let her know that I expected better of her while we were married. I sure as hell will in future."

"Oh, you mean when you told her it was okay that I didn't show up to watch you compete and it was her job to phone and ask me why? I was there, Van. Okay? *I was there.*"

"Where?" His mind went completely blank, white as a bowl of blowing powder.

While her expression crumpled and she buried her face in her trembling hands.

She couldn't mean… He took a few steps toward her, touched her elbow. "Becca."

She dropped her hands and lifted her face. Her eyes were inky pools, so big and filled with pleading for understanding, they were almost cartoonish. His heart lurched, while the cogs in his brain clicked over like the ones in the clock chiming upstairs. Because he knew what she was saying. He knew where she had been. He'd felt her. Looked for her, certain she was there.

"When I raced? You were there when I won?"

"The first gold, yes." She gave a tiny nod, lips clamped together to stop their trembling, chin crinkling.

The important one. The one he'd wanted with every cell in his body.

"Mom said you told her you didn't need a room

at the house. You didn't call me or text to say you were there."

"I stayed somewhere else."

"Where?"

"With people I knew through… It doesn't matter. It was an air bed in a flat full of strangers. That's how I wanted it." She looked down to her hands, knotting them together between them.

"Because of the way Mom and Paisley had been treating you?" He swore under his breath and ran his hand into his hair. "Dad was at a hotel. You could have—" He cut himself off. Everything had been booked years in advance. At best she might have had a pullout sofa in his father's suite and, given what had happened after the games, that was the last place Van would have wanted her to be.

Still.

"Why didn't you tell me? Why didn't you come see me after that race?" He was as dumbfounded and gutted as he'd been when she had failed to emerge from the crowd. He'd pushed through his next races and the team event because he'd trained his whole life to shut out emotional turmoil and focus on the run before him.

And because he'd felt the small lump of her gold heart each time he rubbed the spot above his own.

"I wanted you there, Becca. I understood that your mom needed you and I accepted that's why you stayed away." He had made himself accept it, but to now learn she had been there and hadn't told him? Not even when he came to Sydney? "If you were there, why…" Why had she ended their marriage immediately after? "Did something happen?"

It was starting to compute that something must have, something terrible. There was no other reason she would turn on a dime like that. His stomach filled with concrete.

"What was it?"

She lowered her lashes. "I need to explain a little more about Mum." She rolled her lips in and bit them. "And why she was so sick."

His lungs seized. He had really been hoping she would tell him he was wrong, that nothing had happened.

He waved at the sectional where they had made love hours ago. Where they had made love dozens of times years ago. It now felt like an electric chair as Becca curled defensively into one corner and he took the far end. She faced him, but he looked forward at the blank screen of the TV.

"The reason it took Mum so long to get diagnosed was because she had a rough time with doctors in the past. It had to do with her periods being really painful." She linked her fingers in her lap and tick-ticked her thumbnails against each other. "She was embarrassed to talk about it and when she did, the doctors just, you know, told her to take paracetamol and cuddle a hot water bottle. Long after she had

Wanda, she had a hysterectomy and felt good for the first time since puberty. When she started having pains in her abdomen again, she put off having it looked at, thinking they would treat her like she was still making a fuss over nothing."

"You have painful periods," he recollected. A cold specter seemed to invade his being. "That's why you take your pill without taking a break and try not to have periods at all."

Not if I can help it, she had said the first time he'd realized she hadn't had one. He'd been convinced she was pregnant, but then she had missed a pill while they'd been away for a weekend. When she got her period a week later, she had been doubled over, pale and nauseated, alarming him with how ill she was.

She nodded. "I thought it was kind of normal for it to be so painful. Not *normal*, but every woman complains about it to a different degree. I wasn't suffering every single month the way Mum had so I wasn't abnormal, if that makes sense. Just unlucky. As long as I was on the pill, it was manageable so I did what Mum did and put up with it. But Mum started going for tests while I was still here and that's when she told me, 'It's probably just my endometriosis acting up.' It made me wonder if I had that."

His heart swerved. "Do you?"

"Yes."

A barbed hook caught into him and yanked his soul, tearing a hole in it. "It causes cancer?"

"No! And it's not infectious, either," she hurried to assure him. "You're completely safe."

He shrugged that off, knowing she would have warned him if there were risks to his health. "I'm more concerned about the fact that you were seeing specialists while we were married and you didn't tell me. Have I got that right?"

"Yes." Her profile stiffened.

"No, Becca." He shoved off the sofa and walked away. "Screw training. I had a right to know that you were going for medical tests."

"What was the point in worrying you when I didn't even know what to worry about?"

"Quit saying there was no point to anything. You were the point, Becca. Our marriage was the point."

"Do you want me to tell you what I learned?" Her chin set belligerently. "Or do you want to stand there and yell at me?"

"Talk," he commanded, folding his arms and staying on his feet because he was too agitated to sit again.

She picked at a hangnail. "I was waiting on some results when Dad called and said I had to come home to help Mum. You were in Tahoe and I was homesick."

He flung up a hand.

"Yes, I should have told you that," she said in a beleaguered voice. She drew up her knees and hugged them, letting out a frustrated breath. "It was hard being here alone, Van. I was used to loud bars and chatting with mates at work. Nothing about being here felt right unless you were here, and you never were. The whole time I'd been in Canada, I took for granted that Mum and Dad and Wanda would be there when I was ready to go home, but I suddenly had to face that maybe Mum wouldn't be." She chewed at the corner of her mouth, trying to steady her lips. "So I went home. I had to. That wasn't up for negotiation."

"I know," he said, because he had, but it had still stung that she hadn't waited to see him. That she had kept her medical tests from him.

"I was in Sydney when the ob-gyn finally got back to me."

His fists closed defensively and he wasn't sure why. He moved so he could see her face even though she was balled up like a pill bug, eyes lowered.

"Endometriosis causes scar tissue. Lots of women can still get pregnant when they have it, but the specialist could already tell that it was unlikely I would ever be able to conceive or carry a pregnancy to term. In fact…" She swallowed. "She recommended a partial hysterectomy. I'm putting that off as long as I can because I'm managing for now, but probably before I'm thirty I'll have that done."

Van blinked as if it would clear the dull buzz in his ears. His head felt as though it floated off his body. "Are you saying you can't get pregnant?"

He had heard wrong. She had gotten it wrong. The doctors had. Surely.

She was biting her lips again, brow tense as she nodded.

As he started putting all the pieces together in his head, his chest grew so tight, he could hardly draw a breath. When he swallowed, it felt as though he forced razor blades down his throat. His voice was frayed when he managed to speak.

"You knew this in Sydney when I came to see you? That's why you told me this was all a mistake, that you didn't want to stay married?"

She nodded again.

No.

"I was finished with competing, Becca. I told you I was ready to retire. I wasn't training." His whole body had become pinched in a cage of spikes. "You had no reason to keep that from me. Not then."

"I didn't *want* to tell you." Her eyes flashed up. "I had a lot to deal with, Van. I had just learned my mum was terminal and that I couldn't have kids. I didn't want to believe either of those things." She blinked her matting lashes. "I got that news and had to get on a plane to go watch you race. I could *not* face your family, but I saw you set a record and I was so proud and happy for you. I made my way to the winner's circle to see you and you were with Paisley and the kids and you were holding Flora and looked so…" Her face crumpled.

Van swore and rubbed the place where his breast-bone felt fractured.

"I couldn't talk to you," she choked. "I couldn't make it fit in my head that we would never have a baby of our own."

"Becca—"

"No." She shot to her feet and quickly tightened the belt on her robe. "Don't say there are other ways to make a family. *I know that*. It doesn't mean I wasn't devastated. All I could see was what I couldn't have. Everything was wrong between us, Van. *Everything*. Not just that one thing." She held up a finger.

He couldn't get past the fact that she hadn't told him, though. He was gritting his teeth, chest aching with the hurt of betrayal. "I still deserved to know."

"Oh my God, Van! You came to Sydney and said you were ready to start a family. That's what you said to my *face*." She pointed where the tears brimming her eyes began to roll down her cheeks. "How was I supposed to tell you that was impossible?"

He had said that. He rubbed his hand across his face, feeling as though it was melting off his skull.

"I couldn't, Van. I couldn't say it." All the wind went out of her sails. "And I couldn't keep pretending I was the wife you expected. You brought everything to our marriage—the house and the money and I brought…" She waved at herself. "At least when

I thought I could give you kids I had something to offer, but—"

She turned away and swiped at her cheeks, sniffing back tears.

She was killing him. "Becca." He reached for her.

She shrugged him off. "Don't. Don't say we could have worked it out or found a way." She hugged herself. "This isn't about finding a workaround. It's about me thinking I was being realistic in wanting this one thing. A thing that is supposed to be the reason I exist at all. Getting pregnant is so easy and natural for some women, it happens to them without them even trying. But not me. I don't get that. Do you finally see why I keep my expectations low and refuse to believe in brass rings and fairy tale endings? It's too painful when they don't work out."

Becca didn't wait for his reaction. She moved in a fog to the stairs. *Finish packing*, she thought, distantly aware she was operating on shock-induced autopilot again.

She hadn't wanted to relive the anguish of learning she couldn't get pregnant. Yes, there were long-shot treatments that might allow her to conceive. She had read up on them and understood that she could put herself through all sorts of agonies, emotional and physical, and may or may not carry to term. She didn't want to put herself or Van through any of that.

So, for those first painful months, she'd held the

knowledge inside her like an abscess, letting it eat at her. Eventually she had confided in Wanda, and later the grief counselor who was helping them work through their loss as they cared for Mum. One time, Becca had completely fallen apart at a bus stop and an elderly woman had missed her bus while she sat and listened, then patted her knee.

Living life means feeling the pain of it, the old woman had said. *That's why you have to enjoy what little pleasures there are when they're handed to you.*

She had given Becca a butterscotch candy. Becca still found the taste too bittersweet to bear.

In the bedroom, the bed was wrecked from their antics earlier. Clothes were scattered on the floor… the hair dryer was on the table by the mirror. It looked like she still lived here.

Ignoring the slicing pain that sent through her, she made herself dress in a pair of yoga pants and a T-shirt with a snuggly pullover that did nothing to comfort her. Then she lingered in the closet, staring at the dregs of her life with Van.

Nothing made sense. Nothing. Not meeting him a million years ago, or marrying him, or buying this house and calling it their home and filling it with all these clothes that were too posh or heavy for the life she led in Sydney.

It didn't make sense that she had come here now and he was here and they were saying things that lanced inner boils and left her so drained she felt as though she were bleeding out.

It didn't make sense that she was crying because she had done all her crying. She was sure she had. She had cried when she pushed him away in Sydney and when she had filed the divorce papers. She had cried this morning when she arrived here and smelled him in this closet. She had cried downstairs before they'd made love on the couch.

Her chest was hollow, sobs ringing inside it, throat scorched, eyes swollen. All of her hurt, scalp to toenails. Hurting and hurting and hurting.

She should be finished with it. With all of this. She was divorcing him. Starting fresh. So why was she still hanging on to a white eyelet lace sundress and hugging it to her broken womb as she sank to her knees and fell against the laundry hamper? Why was she aching with loss because she was no longer the woman who had put on this dress with such delusional hopes? She was smarter than that now. Wasn't she?

"Becca."

Weirdly, it made perfect sense that he came in without her hearing him over her storm of heaving sobs, and she wasn't startled at all by his sudden appearance. He gathered up her shuddering body in his strong arms and carried her to the bed and it felt *so right*. Exactly what Van would do because he was perfect and she was not.

"I'm just so sad," she choked. "And I'm so tired of pretending I'm not. When Wanda has kids, she'll have Mum with her again. I never will. And I'll never have your baby and see your eyes or your smile or…"

"Ah, babe. It's not right. It's not." He came with her onto the sheets and aligned her along his strong frame, dragging the covers over them and sheltering her with his whole body.

"I'm sorry," she sobbed into the fuzzy lapel of the robe he still wore, cold fingers petting the line of fine hair against his sternum.

"It's not your fault."

"I mean for all of this. I didn't know how to do any of it. I thought I could fake being your wife and I left when it got hard. That's not love. I know it's not."

"Stop. You're enough, Becca. Okay? Quit thinking you have to be something else. Be you. That's all I ever wanted. Just you."

She didn't even know how to be that. Her. But she was wrecked and exhausted and her eyes were burning with the salt of her tears. She swore these would be the last ones.

CHAPTER TEN

VAN CAREFULLY PUSHED his leg out from beneath the covers, too hot under the comforter with his thick robe and Becca's weight burrowed into his side, but she'd fallen asleep and he wouldn't move more than that, afraid he would disturb her.

He didn't want her to start crying again. Or roll away. He needed to hold her. His chest was a giant ache, as though cleaved open.

Kids. Bloody hell. He'd experienced a certain ambivalence suggesting it to her after the games, but he'd thought that starting a family was something she wanted so he'd been willing. Becca had always been turning her head to smile at babies and toddlers. Kids loved her for the same reason adults did—she gave them her whole attention and made them laugh and feel important.

Van's own feelings toward having a family had been more complicated. He rubbed a tendril of her

hair between his thumb and finger as he acknowledged that.

He'd been confident that Becca would ensure he
was a decent parent, but he hadn't felt any natural
affinity for it, not given the upbringing he'd had. His
mother had never once thought, *Maybe I shouldn't
do this because it will break my kids.* She had simply kept her churn of marriages and affairs with his
coaches and the occasional death threat from an un-
happy wife to herself. Until they leaped out and bit
him.

His mother would say she'd been trying to protect
Van, but it had been a hell of a lot more traumatic to
find out his parents were divorcing through change
room chatter than from her or his father. That's how
it had happened, though.

As for his father… Van blew out a suppressed sigh
toward the ceiling.

Van didn't blame his mother for divorcing Jackson Scott. His father had had wealth and social
standing and an ability to charm when he wanted
something, but he was selfish and jealous and as a father he'd been…absent. When Van looked for a cher-
ished father-son moment, or times when his father
had demonstrated what sort of man Van should become, he drew a blank. All his role models had been
coaches and teachers and the athletes ahead of him.

What scared Van was that he shared his father's
single-mindedness. His drive. Yes, his mother had

possessed a similar focus and stubborn refusal to quit, but Van's father had been cutthroat and very self-involved. When Van looked back, he saw some of that in his own actions, especially when he had married and bought a house and installed Becca inside it, all to please himself.

Van's worst nightmare was that his own kid would wind up feeling about him as he did about his own father—contemptuous. Wanting him out of his life and glad when he was.

He hadn't even considered whether he wanted kids since he'd suggested it to Becca. Given what his own father had done shortly after, Van had shoved parenthood well onto the back burner. It was one of the reasons he hadn't pursued divorce. Yeah, he missed sex, but dating led to marriage and that presumed family, so he'd put off the entire topic.

At least, he had imagined Becca presumed that was their next step. He had wanted to give her what she wanted and he could see now there had been a part of him trying to tie her closer to him, sensing she was pulling away. Besides, why *not* have kids with her? He couldn't think of anything sweeter than a round little face with her dimples and freckles. Her accent spoken in a child's high voice...

Ah, hell. He closed his eyes, trapping the sharp sting that rose behind his lids while he fought to hold back the choke of emotion pressing up from his chest.

After she'd dropped her bomb downstairs and

walked away, he'd stood there trying to read his phone, as if that held the miracle information that would alleviate her suffering.

And his.

Because this was a blow. He breathed through the pain as if it were a physical injury. It was exactly as bad as any broken bone or torn ligament that had ever sidelined him from whatever he had been planning. It hurt like hell to know Becca couldn't get pregnant. And yeah, he knew this wasn't the end for either of them to have a family, but it was the end of something. A dream he hadn't realized he'd harbored close and quiet, barely acknowledging it because it was already so fragile.

Now it was gone. Losing that possibility left a hollow inside him that would be empty and tender all his life.

Becca had been walking around with this ache for years. He'd come up here knowing she would be breaking her heart over it and there she'd been, hiding her grief in the closet like it was something to be ashamed of. Like she wasn't entitled to be angry and hurt by the injustice of it.

He tightened his arms around her, noticing anew how small and soft she was. Becca had such a bright, spicy personality, she always seemed taller and tougher than she really was. Resilient. But she was vulnerable and generous and deserving of every good thing.

I'm just so sad. And I'm so tired of pretending I'm not.

"Me, too," he whispered, nose filling with the tears he was fighting. He rubbed his lips against her satin-smooth forehead. "Me, too."

A loud bang snapped Becca awake. She sat up on a shocked gasp, disoriented by the dark, unfamiliar surroundings, the tangle of blankets and the weight of heavy limbs on hers.

"Fireworks," Van said in a rumble. His hand rubbed her back. "It's midnight."

"Poor dogs," she murmured as there was a *pop-pop-pop* and long hiss. She had once seen a mate's kelpie cower under a sofa and had felt for animals ever since.

She liked watching fireworks herself, though. With a superhuman effort, she dragged herself free of the blankets and walked to the balcony doors, scraping back the drapes to see.

Someone farther down the lakeshore was setting them off. She opened the door and stepped onto the icy, covered balcony, moving to the end where she could lean out to see the bursts of orange and yellow and violet through the falling snow.

Van came out behind her and pulled her back against his chest, wrapping both of them in the comforter he'd brought from the bed.

For ten minutes, they stood there listening to

the whistles and bangs echo across the frozen lake, watching the spirals and explosions flash sparks and color onto the monochrome landscape.

This is it, she thought as another bloomed into feathers of orange fire. It was midnight. There was still paperwork to finish, but in her mind this was the end point. Their marriage was over.

But she stood in the circle of his arms for an extra few minutes, leaning into his chest, heels on his slippers and toes curled against the bite of cold beneath her feet.

She waited until the last spark winked out before she turned to go back inside. She rubbed her feet on the small rug inside the door to dry the damp and work some feeling back into her soles.

Van came in behind her and closed the door. He wafted the comforter back over the bed, then retied his robe.

She didn't know what to say or do. Crawling back into bed so he could put his arms around her sounded appealing, but it would only put off the unavoidable.

She knelt and straightened the few items she'd thrown into the suitcase, making sure the Polaroid photo was in the envelope with the locket before she secured it into a zipped pocket. The rest of the contents were useful, but meaningless.

Van sat on the corner of the bed, elbows on his knees, watching her close the suitcase and stand it up.

"I did fail you," he said with quiet gravity. "The

fact that you felt you couldn't tell me something so important is pure failure on my part."

"Let's be done with pointing fingers and throwing blame. I told you now," she said simply. The tension in her shoulders had dissipated as though a weight had been lifted. "It feels good that you know. I've been carrying it around like it was this great big letdown on my part— No, listen." She held up a hand when he made a noise of protest. "That was how it felt. Like it was my fault our marriage fell apart because my body didn't work the way I wanted it to. I wanted to believe I would have stayed if that hadn't happened, but it was only the final straw."

"It is absolutely not your fault, Becca," he said firmly.

"I know that up here." She tapped her head. "It took a long time to accept it in here." There was still a deep, hollow ache in her chest. Her voice wavered as she added, "Telling you was hard. It makes it real, but hearing you say it's not my fault and not trying to offer to fix me..." She wobbled a smile at him. "That means a lot. Thank you."

He stared at her with incredible intensity, jaw working as though he wanted to say something.

"Yes, I know you would pay for any treatment that would help," she said, biting back an even more tender smile.

"I would," he burst out, shooting to his feet. "That's not about fixing you. You're perfect. I want you to be happy, that's all. Anything that would make you happy, you only have to tell me and I'll do whatever I can."

He was going to make her cry again and she was done with tears, she really was, but oh, he was a very sweet, good man.

"I know, Van. Thank you." She swallowed down her emotion and stood.

She moved to hug him. *Last one*, she promised herself as his arms folded tight around her. His heart thudded heavily against her ear. They made the tiny adjustments so they fit just so. She closed her eyes and hung on to him for a long time, long enough she forgot they were standing until he rubbed her back.

"Let's get to bed," he said gruffly. "You're falling asleep on your feet."

Pulling away caused a visceral tearing sensation down her front. She made herself breathe through the pain and concentrate on pressing back the hot tears behind her eyes.

With a nod of agreement, she moved the suitcase into the hall.

"Where are you going?" He frowned.

"The spare room."

"Stay here." He waved at the bed.

"It's your house now, Van. Your bed." Her emotions were all over the place, heart feeling flattened and smeared.

"I mean *stay* here," he said more forcefully. "The

fact that you can't get pregnant changes nothing. I don't know if *I* can make babies. Did you think of that? We'll figure out how to have a family if and when the time is right. I'm still coming to Australia, Becca. We're staying married."

"Your presumption that you can have anything you want is astounding." She swiped the heel of her hand beneath her eyes. She kind of loved him all the more for it. It was inspiring. She definitely ought to become more like him if she wanted to be happy. "I want this to be easy, Van. Can you at least give me that?"

"You want me to give you up without a fight? That's really what you want from me?"

His voice was jagged with offense, the line of his shoulders iron straight and rock hard. "I don't know how to give up, Becca."

The irony didn't escape her. She was asking a man who never surrendered to do just that. She wanted him to give her what she wanted, and it was a loss so deep she didn't expect she would ever fully recover from it. In fact, she knew she wouldn't. She hadn't gotten over him in four years so she doubted she would feel any better tomorrow or the next day or the next.

Nevertheless, she made herself say, "Yes."

"You won't give us one more chance," he scoffed with disbelief. *"One."*

"Van." Her voice was gentle. She couldn't even

be angry with him anymore. All the fuel for hurt and resentment had been burned away by the fire of brutal honesty that had roared between them over the last hours. There was only one last hot, painful lick of truth. "We *never* had a chance. We had great sex and good laughs, but you didn't love me. When I told you I loved you, you got that look right there."

His entire demeanor hardened as if warding off this final, troubling fact.

"You didn't believe me when I said it. You thought after all this time I was coming back to steal from you. If you want me to say things I should have said four years ago…" Her throat tried to close. She clung to her elbows, too adrift to feel anything but loss. "After I learned I couldn't give you a baby, love was all I had to offer you. But you didn't *want* my love. How the hell could you expect me to stay married to that?"

CHAPTER ELEVEN

BECCA WOKE TO the sort of morning she had always loved in Canada. The sky was so blue as to pierce the eyes, the sun opening like an eye in the notch of the mountains, casting beams and sparks and glittering promise in every direction.

Overnight, the wind had quit churning the snow. Like her emotions, all was settled into a thick blanket of calm. The world was unmarred and quiet. A blank slate. No mistakes yet made. New day, new year.

New Becca.

She looked to the closed door of the master bedroom, but didn't walk down to knock on it for a final goodbye. They had said all that needed to be said. She touched her fingertips to her lips in a softly blown kiss and tiptoed downstairs with her nearly empty suitcase.

The kitchen was a disaster zone. She used her app to book a rideshare and quietly loaded the dishwasher while she waited, then sat down to write her card to Van.

A million things had run through her mind when she'd bought it, nothing feeling right. She had thought there would be apologies to make, but she wasn't sorry, that's what she realized as she sat there staring at the white card. She was glad she'd been married to him. Glad to have known him. Glad they had had this final night to bandage up old hurts. Now they could both move on and heal.

There was only one thing left to say.

I love you. I always will.

She glanced at the app and hurried to put on her boots and coat, and grabbed the suitcase and her purse before she rushed out into the bracing cold. The dry air made her nose sting and her eyes water. This was the kind of day she loved to look at, she thought wryly. Preferably from a hot bath or beneath the down comforter on the bed with a naked Van beside her.

He would be happy when he hit the slopes later, though. This was what he called champagne powder, so dry it didn't even melt as it coated her jeans.

It made for a heavy slog, though, reaching as high as her thighs in some places. She worked up a sweat as she hoofed through it. Her breath was fogging, lungs aching as she very ungracefully grunted her way up the hill toward the gate.

The car appeared at the top and honked. She waved and hop-stepped, trying to run, but it was no use. At least the driver saw her and sent a friendly wave.

Still, with someone waiting she had enough sense of urgency she wasn't tempted to look back.

Van woke to a profound sense of absence, one that left a resounding echo inside him. She was gone; he knew she was.

He sat up, angry with himself because he hadn't meant to fall asleep. He'd been sitting on the bed, hearing her say it again and again.

You didn't want my love. How the hell could you expect me to stay married to that?

He hadn't known what to say because it was true. Every time she'd told him she loved him, he'd felt those words as an obligation she was placing on him. All his life, love had been a transaction. His parents, coaches, even fans had only ever said they loved him because he won. Shareholders loved him because he made them money and his sister, well, theirs was a comrade-in-arms sort of love that demanded he always be at her disposal because she didn't believe in that emotion any more than he did.

Unconditional love simply didn't exist in his world. It was a unicorn, just like Becca. He had never been able to figure out what she wanted from him in exchange for this outpouring of acceptance she offered. He had given her jewelry and a dream home and the ability to stay in this country, all the while aware she really wanted his time, but when he'd finally offered her that, she'd rebuffed him.

It still turned a knife in his belly.

He'd done the same thing last night, offering his time and his money and his support. Whatever she wanted. He just wanted her in his life.

But it wasn't enough for her.

Love was all I had to offer you. You didn't believe me when I said it.

He hadn't. He had wanted to, but he hadn't. Now he was sorry. He should have seen her love for the gift it was and kept it. Protected it and hoarded it because now he'd lost it for good and that made for a very bleak future.

He rose from the bed feeling as though he'd lived a thousand years overnight. As though he had been partying and was suffering the worst hangover of his life.

He tightened the belt on the robe and blinked his gritty eyes at the belligerently beautiful day. As he stepped out of the bedroom and glanced down to the guest room, he saw the bed didn't even look slept in. Downstairs, the kitchen was clean.

It was almost as though her presence here had been nothing more than a prurient fantasy and a tragic dream—if not for the card she'd left propped against the cold candle on the dining table.

His hesitated as he reached for it, wanting to know what she had said, but not sure he could bear it. It was probably still blank. They'd said everything they had needed to say.

Hadn't they?

As he opened it, he heard a distant honk of a car horn.

"Beccaaaa!" A door slammed in the distance.

She stopped at the gate, out of breath, jeans clammy and coated with snow to above her knees. Her fingers ached where they fumbled with the icy metal clasp. The rideshare car was running its exhaust and she gave a wave to brush the fumes from her face.

"Becca, damn you, don't leave." Van's voice was so angry, she was tempted to make a run for it in reaction.

She stood frozen in place as he appeared at the bottom of the drive.

He still wore his robe and nothing else but a pair of unlaced boots. The robe was pulling open as he ran so that—

"Van. For heaven's sake." She motioned for him to close the robe. "You'll catch pneumonia." And start rumors that most men found unflattering, given how the brisk winter air was liable to affect him. "What's wrong? Did I forget something?"

"Yes." He was clomping up to her with way more agility than she'd had even though he was practically naked. Snow had to be falling into his unlaced boots, but he didn't seem to care. His hair was disheveled, his jaw unshaved. He looked like a grouchy, shaggy bear awakened early from hibernation.

"What?" She left her suitcase at the gate and motioned to the driver for patience as she tromped back toward Van.

His breath gusted out in big clouds as his chest heaved from the exertion of coming after her. He was twitching with shivers as he thrust out the card she'd left him.

"Van…" she trailed off helplessly. "I wanted you to know that…"

"Open it."

She did, cautiously, and saw her own words. That's all. Nothing else.

Her heart had swooped up so incredibly fast with hope. Now it fell just as swiftly, landing hard. Tears of disappointment sprang to her eyes.

"Why—?"

"I want this, Becca." He pointed at the card. "This love of yours is *mine*. I want it more than I want anything else in this world. But I have to give it back to you. Right? That's how this works? You give me yours. I give you mine?"

"But you *don't* love me, Van."

"Don't you doubt me," he said with affront. "We're not repeating old mistakes. Remember?" He clomped a step closer and cupped her cold cheeks in his cold hands, looked deep into her eyes. "You are the only woman I want. I'm selling this house because what is the use in having it if you're not in it? I don't know how to love except by…" He shrugged and looked at their surroundings. "By giving you everything I have. I didn't think words *could* be enough." His brow flexed. "But if that's what you need, if that's *all* you need, then you have them. As much as you mean those words, so do I. *I love you. I always will.*"

She had never fainted in her life, but she almost did right then. Her heart took a hard bounce and she forgot to breathe and her vision tunneled into pinpoints so all she saw was him. His warm hands cupping her cheeks was the only thing holding her upright.

"Don't say it's too much," he warned gruffly. "I don't know how to give you enough love."

Her eyes were watering so hard she had to blink to clear her vision. "It does feels like too much. It does," she choked. "Because I'm…"

"Be careful what you say next, love." His hands gentled. His thumbs settled at the corners of her mouth and his lips touched the tip of her numb nose. "I have very high standards and I will not take kindly to hearing that my wife is anything less than utterly amazing."

She tilted a wet look up at him and the sunlight glinting through the trees turned everything into halos and sparkling light. The world was silent and the air crisp and fresh. The moment too big with possibility.

"I'm scared," she admitted in a whisper.

"Me, too. But I can't do another four years without you. I can't do four minutes."

Behind her, the driver opened his car door. "You folks hosting a polar bear swim?"

"No," Van called absently, gaze locked to hers. "But that's how I've felt since you were gone, like I was naked in a frozen lake. *Come back.*"

Hard shivers were chasing through his body, but he didn't mean she should come back in the house to warm up. He meant forever.

Be smart, Becca. You might get your heart broken again.

Or she might not. She wouldn't know if she didn't try. Maybe she could have things other people got.

Or maybe she could have this one thing that no one else had—Van's love.

She began to tremble, but it might have been shivers. She nodded jerkily.

Van grabbed her shoulders and planted a kiss on her lips, a hard, hurried one that was no less powerful for its brevity.

Then he released her and brushed past her, grabbing up her suitcase as he told the driver, "She's staying with me, but don't knock her rating. Do you ski?" Van quickly had the man grinning at the news that he could pick up a full complement of Van Scott gear from a local shop.

As the car drove away, she and Van slipped and

skittered down to the house, laughing and clinging to each other.

"I swear, if you locked us out of the house…"

"I might have. I wasn't thinking of anything but catching you."

The door was open and they tumbled in, kissing and falling into each other's arms. It was exciting and sweet and so achingly good, she couldn't help pausing and sobering.

"Is this happening too fast?"

"Probably. That's how we do things." He rubbed her arms.

"That's how you do things," she said pointedly.

"It's okay if you need time, Becca. It is." He dipped his head to look straight into her eyes. "But *tell* me if that's what you need. Don't shut me out, okay? Not again. Promise?"

She gave a faltering nod. "You, neither."

"Open book. I swear."

They kissed with their still-cold lips, but it was sweet and hopeful and made her want to believe in this. That she could have him. That they could be like this forever.

He was still shivering, and she slithered her arms inside his robe to try to warm him. Her clothes were cold and the snow clinging to her jeans was melting and damp, making him flinch and pull away with a laugh.

"Look, I know I *just* said I wouldn't rush you." He

winked one eye as though he suspected he was pushing his luck. "But I need to warm up. Any chance
you want to join me in a hot shower?"

"Is the sauna still on standby?"

"Oh, yeah, let's do that."

Van changed her flight so Becca could stay a few
extra days in Whistler and they could travel together
to Sydney. Becca had given a private eye roll when
he upgraded her ticket to first class, but also gave a
private squeal of glee because she'd never had the
promise of free champagne when she boarded before.

They were leaving tomorrow, and she was already
second-guessing her school plan, but Van insisted he
would live his life around hers while she started her
classes to see if lab work would be a good fit for her.

These few days of reconciliation were almost too
ideal. They skied and made love and talked about
everything and nothing, but she kept having faltering moments of worrying it couldn't last. She feared
she would come crashing back to earth any second.

Each time it happened, Van seemed to notice,
catching at her hand or saying a quiet, "Hey. You
know I love you, right?" And when he said it, he
pulled her into his arms and held her like she was
the most precious thing in the universe.

He wanted to remarry in Sydney, but with a
proper wedding with both families in attendance.

"I'm sorry we didn't do it right the first time, so your mom could be there. Let's do better this time."

"Your family doesn't want to come all that way for a second marriage," Becca protested as they left a pub where they'd just had lunch.

"Are you kidding? Paisley is dying for an excuse to bring the kids—wait. We're not going home yet." He drew her in a different direction from his SUV. "This is why I wanted to have lunch here. I need to go across the street."

She tugged him to a halt as he led her toward a jewelry store.

"Please don't buy me new rings. I like these." She adjusted hers on her finger.

"So do I." He wore his wedding band, too, even though their arrangements with their lawyers meant a certificate of divorce would appear in roughly a month. "This is something else."

"My locket? You got it fixed?" She hadn't wanted to give it up, preferring to take it home to get it repaired so she wouldn't risk leaving it here again, but Van had sheepishly confessed how he'd broken it—turning her inside out with love for him. He had insisted on ensuring it was mended so she had tentatively entrusted it to him again.

Now he was giving her a cagey look that made her tense with apprehension as she went through the door he held.

The upscale shop was full of custom items. Van

gave his name and the clerk disappeared. She came
back with a small velvet box and a big smile.

"I saw the goldsmith working on this. What a
lovely idea."

"Thanks. Would you give us a minute?" he asked
in the most charming "shove off" in history.

As the woman walked away, Van opened the lid,
still eyeing Becca as though he wasn't sure how she
would react.

She looked down and saw her locket, mended and
encased in a bigger heart-shaped locket with a glass
front. A plethora of diamonds embedded the gold
border of the larger one and it hung off a chain that
looked like braided gold.

"Van," she breathed, absently touching her empty
neck.

"I was worried about your little heart getting all
banged up again. I want to protect it with my own."

She bit lips that began to tremble with an emo-
tive smile.

He took the necklace from the box, holding it up
as he opened the clasp. "You can see right into mine.
And you could break it," he warned somberly. "But
I know you won't. Not on purpose. That's why I'm
trusting you with it."

"You…" She didn't have words. She was blinking hard so she could continue to see and lifted her
hair to let him put it on her. It was a cool, tickling
weight accompanied by a soft kiss against her nape.

Across the room, she saw a blurry pair of women with their heads together, hands on their chests.

"You like it?" Van asked as she turned back to him.

"I love it so much I don't even know what to say." She shifted so she could see it in the mirror, but was still trying to clear her matted lashes.

"Say you'll keep it always."

"Always," she vowed, learning the shape of it with her touch, enjoying the press of it on her throat. It was a heavy, extravagant statement that was proof he understood what was most important to her. It was utterly priceless. "I'll take such good care of it. I promise."

He turned her and nudged it a millimeter to center it, then cupped her neck and swooped his mouth down to hers in one of his heady, mind-bending kisses. Her eyes burned and he sent her soaring with joy.

Maybe this was what love really was, she thought fleetingly. Sometimes it was a hard shell that kept you safe, other times it was a dangerous fishtail that thrilled and blinded and left you breathless.

Maybe that's just who they were and maybe that was perfectly fine.

EPILOGUE

Five years later

"MY TEACHER SAID there's no such thing as second birthday." Liam blinked his big brown eyes behind his thick glasses. "Only if you're two. I'm five." His free hand starfished while he kept a firm hold of Van's fingers with his other one.

"I know, son. Your teacher is right." Van's heart turned over with love for the boy. He wanted to pick him up and squeeze him, but they were working on respecting personal space at school. There was a time and place for wrestling, and a jewelry store wasn't it. "That's just what your mom calls it and it's really for her."

"Is that why we're getting her a present?"

"Yeah. Can you hold your thumb while we're in here or do you want to hold my hand?" Van held the door open.

"I can just look."

"That's what I thought. You're the best kid in the world. Did you know that?"

Liam nodded his floppy hair because, yeah, of course he was the best kid in the world. His parents had been telling him that as long as he could remember.

He'd been quite a handful in the beginning. Becca had wanted to try a foster-to-adopt situation, which Van had completely supported even though he had privately worried that Becca would get her heart broken if something went awry. Hell, he'd been worried he would, once he'd met this little rascal. They'd all fallen in love immediately.

Liam had been two, which was always a challenging age. He'd been affectionate and curious, but his lively and sometimes stubborn nature had become more than his grandparents could handle, especially after suffering the loss of his mom.

At that time, Liam had grabbed *everything*. Often, he had impulsively run to look at something that caught his eye, not paying attention to his surroundings and putting himself in danger when he did. He'd constantly been tripping and tumbling and keeping Van and Becca on guard.

One day, when Liam had stood in front of the television refusing to move, Becca had said, "Do you think he has trouble seeing?"

They'd booked him an appointment and within a couple of weeks, the boy had been wearing a pair of thick glasses. He had still grabbed for everything in his reach, but once his depth perception improved, he wasn't knocking things over as he did. When they read to him, he began pointing out animals, mimicking the sounds. Words quickly followed and being able to make himself understood had made his tantrums mostly obsolete.

It was a bittersweet victory. As his behavior improved, they were sure his grandparents would change their minds about relinquishing him to adoption. Instead, they agreed to an open situation and still took Liam for a weekend every month or two, joining Van and Becca for Liam's birthday and Christmas and any other occasion when family was gathering. Becca and his grandmother were really close, both having a hole in their life that the other filled in her own way.

Van was glancing over earrings and bracelets, conscious that Becca wouldn't expect or particularly want anything expensive, but the anniversary of Liam's adoption was important to him, too. He wanted to mark it with something special.

"Daddy, that one's a plabbidus." Liam kept hold of his thumb while he pointed at some crystal figurines. "Mummy would like it."

Van came to look at the modest little sculpture of a platypus, always getting a kick out of the way Liam mixed up his words and imbued a few with Becca's accent. Maybe they hadn't made him, but he definitely reflected bits of both of them. The boy had taken to skiing like a duck to water last winter.

"She would, wouldn't she?" Becca would love it because her son had picked it out.

They had visited Becca's family twice since Liam had joined them and both trips had included visits to the zoo with Wanda's kids. Wanda was bringing her family this Christmas, excited for her kids to see snow for the first time.

Van nodded at the clerk to wrap it, and thirty minutes later, they entered the house to the scent of angel food cake. It would only be the three of them, but all the more special for being an intimate celebration.

Becca had already changed out of the floral scrubs she wore to the lab and waved, pointing to show him she was on the phone with the Bluetooth.

She worked at the lab on a casual basis, also running a foundation funded by Van Scott Equipment that ensured underprivileged kids could learn to ski. Van mostly worked from home and scrupulously limited his hours, keeping his schedule flexible so he could pick up Liam from school when Becca had commitments of her own.

"My husband just walked in," she said to whoever she was talking to. "Let me discuss it with him. We'll call you back in the next day or so? Yes, thank you." She hung up.

"Bec. Are you crying?" Van moved to take her

arms, blood chilling in his veins as he noted the redness around her eyes. "What happened?"

"I'm fine. I promise." She beamed him a smile through her misty eyes and patted his chest, giving him a distracted kiss before quickly bending to reassure Liam. "I missed you while I was at work today. Where have you and Daddy been? How come you're late getting home from school?"

"We got you a present." He proudly offered the gold-embossed bag.

"Goodness! That wasn't necessary." She gave Van a you-shouldn't-have look and weighed it. "I wonder what it could be."

"A plabbidus."

"Oh. Does he need water?"

"Not a real one!" Liam said with a giggle.

She chuckled and hugged him again, gaze soft with love. "I can't wait to see it, but I'll open it after tea, if that's okay. Do you want a few minutes of screen time? I need to talk to Daddy."

Liam nodded and she set the timer on his tablet, sending him toward the stairs where he had a playroom in the loft.

"Who was it?" Van asked with concern as Liam started up the stairs.

"Tamara," she said in a lowered voice, mentioning the social worker who had assisted with their adoption of Liam. "There's a little girl she thinks would be a good fit for us."

"Babe." It was a heart-punch of hope.

Van took her trembling form into his arms. They had planned to wait a little longer before bringing another child into their lives, worried about risking Liam growing attached to someone who might not be able to stay. Van was trying to be patient, but he really wanted to fill out their family.

"I know what you're going to say. It's always risky," she pointed out. "This little girl only has an elderly grandfather who wants to be in the picture, but can't take custody of her. It wouldn't be a foster situation. We could adopt her right away. She's three and has a small health concern that requires injections which was one reason Tamara thought of us. That, and we already have the open situation with Liam's family so she knows we understand that dynamic. I know we said we'd wait a little longer before we made any moves, but…" She raised a pleading gaze to his. "I really want Liam to have a little sister. She could be with us by Thanksgiving."

"I want a little sister," Liam said. He had only gone midway up the stairs and sat there, tablet held in two hands before him.

Van couldn't help a guffaw at the kid refusing to be left out of a private conversation. Or not having his vote counted on something so important to all of them.

"Sounds like three out of three," Van said wryly, hugging Becca tight. "Motion carried to proceed?"

By Christmas, their daughter Sarah was with them. She was round and assertive and still getting used to her new family. When Wanda offered her a gift to unwrap, she grew overwhelmed by her new cousins and all the noise as they tore into presents with Liam.

"Sarah, come sit with Mummy, love," Becca invited, opening her arms.

Sarah quickly took refuge in her mother's lap. She absently played with the pendant at Becca's throat as they watched all the action from a safe place in the corner of the sofa. Becca accepted the gift from Wanda and they opened it together, admiring the puzzle of marsupials it contained.

"Hey." Van waited for Becca to lift her shining eyes before he snapped his photo. "You look really beautiful."

She wrinkled her nose, but didn't protest that she was in rumpled pajamas with uncombed hair. She hadn't had much sleep, either. She'd been up late with her sister, wrapping presents, then the house had been awaked early by excited children who wanted to know if Santa had come.

"I'm happy," she told him. "It's the best makeup there is."

"That's all I wanted for Christmas. Ever, really."

"And you got what you wanted? There's a surprise." She was teasing him, sifting fingers through their daughter's hair and kissing the girl's brow while wearing the most incandescent expression he'd ever seen.

He would have taken another photo to capture that look, but he saw it often enough he was just as satisfied to shift across and kiss her instead.

* * * * *

If you thought
One Snowbound New Year's Night
was magical
you're sure to love these other stories
by Dani Collins!

What the Greek's Wife Needs
Ways to Ruin a Royal Reputation
Her Impossible Baby Bombshell
Married for One Reason Only
Manhattan's Most Scandalous Reunion

Available now!

#3977 PROMOTED TO THE GREEK'S WIFE
The Stefanos Legacy
by Lynne Graham

Receptionist Cleo's attraction to billionaire Ari Stefanos is a fiercely kept secret. Until one sizzling night it's deliciously exposed! But when Ari needs a bride to help claim his orphaned niece, their simmering connection makes accepting his ring very complicated!

#3978 THE SCANDAL THAT MADE HER HIS QUEEN
Pregnant Princesses
by Caitlin Crews

One scandalous encounter with Crown Prince Zeus has left Nina penniless and pregnant. She's not expecting anything from Zeus aside from his protection. Certainly not a marriage proposal! Or for their desire to reignite—hot, fast and dangerous...

#3979 THE CEO'S IMPOSSIBLE HEIR
Secrets of Billionaire Siblings
by Heidi Rice

Ross is in for a shock when he's reunited with the unforgettable Carmel—and sees a child who looks undeniably like him! Now that the truth is revealed, can Ross prove he'll step up for Carmel and their son?

#3980 HIS SECRETLY PREGNANT CINDERELLA
by Millie Adams

When innocent Morgan is betrayed by Constantine's brother, the last thing she expects is an explosion of forbidden chemistry between her and Constantine. Now a bump threatens to reveal the twin consequences, and Constantine will do everything to claim them!

#3981 FORBIDDEN NIGHTS IN BARCELONA
The Cinderella Sisters
by Clare Connelly
Set aflame by the touch of totally off-limits Alejandro Corderó, Sienna does the unthinkable and proposes they have a secret week of sensual surrender in Barcelona. But an awakening under the Spanish sun may prove seven nights won't be enough...

#3982 SNOWBOUND IN HIS BILLION-DOLLAR BED
by Kali Anthony
Running from heartbreak and caught in a bitter snowstorm, Lucy's forced to seek shelter in reclusive Count Stefano's castle. Soon, she finds herself longing to unravel the truth behind his solitude and the searing heat promised in his bed...

#3983 CLAIMING HIS VIRGIN PRINCESS
Royal Scandals
by Annie West
Hounded by the paparazzi after two failed engagements, Princess Isla of Altbourg escapes to Monaco. She'll finally let her hair down in private. Perhaps irresistible self-made Australian billionaire Noah Carson can help...?

#3984 DESERT PRINCE'S DEFIANT BRIDE
by Julieanne Howells
A pretend engagement to Crown Prince Khaled wasn't part of Lily's plan to prove her brother's innocence, but the brooding sheikh is quite insistent. Their simmering chemistry makes playing his fiancée in public easy—and resisting temptation in private impossible!
